MONKEY

A Pandora *Whodunnit*

Miles Franklin was born in 1879 on a property near Tumut, New South Wales, and grew up in the Goulburn district. At the age of sixteen she wrote her first and most famous novel, *My Brilliant Career*, which is now a successful film. Miles Franklin was a strong and independent woman and a strong feminist. Between 1905 and 1914 she lived in the United States, where she worked in the women's labour movement and co-edited *Life and Labour*. During the First World War, she was an honorary helper in England and an orderly to the Scottish Women's Hospital in Macedonia. She continued to write until her death in September 1954.

PANDORA

London and New York

BRING THE MONKEY

MILES FRANKLIN

With an introduction by Bronwen Levy

PANDORA

London and New York

This edition first published in 1987 by
Pandora Press
(Routledge & Kegan Paul Ltd)
11 New Fetter Lane, London EC4P 4EE

Published in USA by
Routledge & Kegan Paul Inc.
in association with Methuen Inc.
29 West 35th Street, New York, NY 10001

Set in Linotron Sabon 10 on 11½ point
by Input Typesetting London SW19 8DR
Printed in Great Britain
by Cox & Wyman Ltd., Reading

British Library Cataloguing in Publication Data

Franklin, Miles
Bring the monkey.—(Pandora women
crime writers).
I. Title
823 [F]   PR9619.3.F68
ISBN 0 86358 199-4

Pandora Women Crime Writers

Series editors: Rosalind Coward and Linda Semple

In introducing the *Pandora Women Crime Writers* series we have two aims: to reprint the best of women crime writers who have disappeared from print and to introduce a new generation of women crime writers to all devotees of its genre. We also hope to seduce new readers to the pleasures of detective fiction.

Women have used the tradition of crime writing inventively since the end of the last century. Indeed, in many periods women have dominated crime writing, as in the so-called Golden Age of detective fiction, usually defined as between the first novel of Agatha Christie and the last of Dorothy L. Sayers. Often the most popular novels of the day, and those thought to be the best in their genre, were written by women. But as in so many areas of women's writing, many of these have been allowed to go out of print. Few people know the names of Josephine Bell, Pamela Branch, Hilda Lawrence, Marion Mainwaring or Anthony Gilbert (whose real name was Lucy Malleson). Their novels are just as good and entertaining as when they were first written.

Women's importance in the field of crime writing is just as vital today. P. D. James, Ruth Rendell and Patricia Highsmith have all ensured that crime writing is treated seriously. Not so well known, but equally flourishing, is a new branch of feminist crime writers. We plan to introduce many new writers from this area, from England and other countries.

The integration of reprints and the new feminist novels is

sometimes uneasy. Some writers do make snobbish, even racist remarks. However it is a popular misconception that all earlier novels are always snobbish and racist. Many of our chosen and favourite authors managed to avoid, sometimes deliberately, the prevailing views. Others are more rooted in the ideologies of their time and when their remarks jar, it does serve to remind us that any novel must be understood by reference to the historical context in which it was written.

Some of the best writers who will be appearing in this series are: Josephine Bell, Ina Bouman, Christianna Brand, Pamela Branch, Katherine V. Forrest, Miles Franklin, Anthony Gilbert (Lucy Malleson), Hilda Lawrence, Marion Mainwaring, Sara Shulman, Nancy Spain.

Linda Semple
Rosalind Coward

The first novels to be published during 1987 are:

Green for Danger by Christianna Brand
Death of a Doll by Hilda Lawrence
Murder in Pastiche by Marion Mainwaring
and
Amateur City by Katherine V. Forrest

Our autumn 1987 titles are:

Bring the Monkey by Miles Franklin
The Port of London Murders by Josephine Bell
The Spinster's Secret by Anthony Gilbert (Lucy Malleson)
and
Murder at the Nightwood Bar by Katherine V. Forrest

To JEAN and PETER
in memory of
variegated and heartwarming
experiences
London, 1932

INTRODUCTION

'What a lark to publish a detective story by Miles Franklin.'[1]
So said P.R. (Inky) Stephensen whose new and short-lived
Endeavour Press published *Bring the Monkey* in Sydney in
1933. Norman Lindsay, who was manuscript reader for
Endeavour, was delighted with the novel and provided a
jacket illustration.[2] It was a nice coincidence that Franklin
had depicted her narrator reading a Lindsay book (p. 244).

In 1933 Franklin was fifty-two years old and had recently
returned to Australia to live after twenty-six years' residence
overseas, chiefly in Chicago and in London. She was pleased
to be associated with the Endeavour Press, which was a
subsidiary of the *Bulletin* and which Stephensen envisaged as
promoting Australian writing. Unfortunately, the Press was
plagued with difficulties during its short existence from 1932
to 1935. For Stephensen, one problem was the quality of
printing available at the *Bulletin*, and *Bring the Monkey* was
the only Endeavour publication that he succeeded in having
printed elsewhere.[3] For the novel to be published by
Endeavour, Franklin first had to buy the copyright from the
receiver of the London publisher, Cecil Palmer, who had
bought the manuscript when Franklin was in London but
had subsequently gone bankrupt.

Franklin described *Bring the Monkey* as a 'light novel'. She
reported that 'The book has had a joyous welcome from
Queensland to New Zealand and south and west to Perth.'[4]
Nettie Palmer thought it a 'slashing detective story' and
commented that it 'represents one side of its author's
temperament . . . and contains, as *obiter dicta*, certain inter-

esting comments that nobody else would have made.'[5] The novel is a satire of murder mysteries set in British country houses and of British comedies of the ilk of those by Noel Coward and Evelyn Waugh. For Marjorie Barnard, it is 'a satire of a satire of a satire, a thriller to end all thrillers'.[6]

Light entertainment notwithstanding, *Bring the Monkey* was written by Miles Franklin and so will be read in the light of its authorship. Sometimes the reader will be beckoned to forsake the clues in the mystery story in favour of speculation about the novel's place in its author's literary production. *Bring the Monkey* was published under the same name as *My Brilliant Career* – 'Miles Franklin', part of her full name, Stella Maria Sarah Miles Franklin, and originally adopted to hide her female identity. Here, Franklin does not seek the protection of pseudonyms such as 'Mr and Mrs Ogniblat l'Artsau' (Talbingo Austral[ia]), used for *The Net of Circumstance*, a light romance published in 1915, or 'Brent of Bin Bin', used for much of her later work. A writer like Franklin who delighted in her various pseudonyms must have enjoyed writing a mystery with plenty of assumed identities and unlikely disguises. Franklin had herself once masqueraded as a housemaid for a few weeks and she depicts the narrator in *Bring the Monkey* adopting a housemaid identity.

Readers of *My Brilliant Career* and the Bin Bin novels may be surprised to find in *Bring the Monkey* a novel so different from her other work. The years of Franklin's 'middle period' – those spent overseas – seem, however, to have been marked by a search on her part for literary forms and themes. Under various names, she wrote novels, plays and stories, some of which remain unpublished or out of print, despite the recent revival of interest in her work. She may well have written stories for *Life and Labor*, the monthly magazine of the National Women's Trade Union League on which she worked with Alice Henry and others in Chicago.[7] These years appear to have been disappointing in terms of her literary success and, ultimately, also confusing in terms of her politics. When Franklin left Australia in 1906, she was a feminist and a nationalist, a champion of the underdog. In the United States, she worked for the cause of working women. But the jingoistic militarism of World War I was the distressing outcome of nationalism like Franklin's and, when she left Chicago for London in 1915, her cross-class feminism was in conflict with the socialist of working-class women. The historical circumstances of the 1920s, 1930s and 1940s could not resolve these contradictions for Franklin although throughout her life she remained a committed feminist.[8]

Franklin's feminist politics led to many strong friendships with women. Through one of these, she was introduced to the central character of this novel, Percy the monkey. In real life Peter the monkey, he belonged to Mabel Singleton who shared a flat in London in High Street, Kensington with Franklin and with Mary Fullerton, also an expatriate Australian novelist and one of the few to know the identity of Brent of Bin Bin. Fullerton is probably the 'M.F.' in the dedication of the 1931 Bin Bin novel, *Back to Bool Bool*. *Bring the Monkey* is dedicated to Peter (the monkey) and to Jean Hamilton, another person in on the Brent secret who, like Fullerton, acted as an intermediary between Franklin as Brent of Bin Bin and her publishers.

Like his fictional representation, Peter the monkey had engaging if mischievous ways. In the novel, he is presented as intelligent, a dainty creature with 'fairy' (p. 146) hands, cleaner and more likeable than the 'mangy' cats and dogs beloved by the old women the narrator calls 'poor old potties' (p. 82). Unruly manners temper a monkey's charms, however. Winifred Stephensen made Peter's acquaintance with her publisher husband Inky and wrote in her diary thus:

> (at dinner) 'Peter the monkey has some pretty ways, but a great strain on one's nerves. He bit me and Inky asked for iodine.'
> (in Hyde Park, London) '. . . we were followed by an assorted crowd as I've no doubt they thought us members of a circus.'[9]

Events of a like nature gave Franklin the humorous starting point for this novel and helped to structure its action. But even as light fiction, *Bring the Monkey* is also informed by its author's personal and political experience. For the Franklin enthusiast, the way such experience is mediated in a light satirical thriller offers a fascinating contrast to her other various works.

The satire in *Bring the Monkey* depends to a large extent on the status of the narrator and her friend, Zarl, as outsiders. As a 'cool plucky pair of young women' (p. 79) from Australia, they are free to observe the British system without fully participating in it. At the same time, their author can offer a satirical version, with strong feminist overtones, of the conventions of British country house comedies and of British mystery thrillers of 'the butler did it' type. Unlike the villain, Zarl and her friend are neither male nor upper class nor English – the rot starts within the system in this novel. Their association with Percy the monkey helps them get an invitation to the houseparty and, in the end, they manage to evade the restrictions placed on them by their situation. Even Percy is an exotic, a 'little exile from glorious African sunshine' (p. 112) that is notoriously missing in damp, grey England.

For Australian readers of the 1930s, poking fun at the habits of the English aristocracy may have contributed to the novel's appeal (although some Australian customs are satirized too). For example, the narrator decides that the rich and famous houseguests are 'as well-groomed as prize beasts at a fair, but most of them petty or mediocre or worse under test' (p. 66). Franklin's nationalism does not always lead to such egalitarianism, however. If she was a loyal Australian she was also a loyal Britisher and so, while she mocked the English class system she also, like many others in the 1930s, harboured racist and anti-semitic attitudes. The resulting racist overtones in her work include, in *Bring the Monkey*, the Indian character, Yusuf, who functions in a similar way to the stock black comic figures in other works of the period. He is said, for instance, to sniff loudly and impolitely in the British Museum Reading Room.

While the novel's racism may be dated, it raises questions for Australian feminists who have assisted in the current revival of interest in Franklin's works, particularly following the film of *My Brilliant Career*. The contradictions posed by questions of race and class for what had previously appeared to be egalitarian feminist politics led to Franklin's eventual disillusionment with organized politics altogether. Similar contradictions have not been adequately resolved in contemporary feminism. Other aspects of the novel's politics, such as its anti-militarism, may be more appealing to contemporary readers. The villain of the piece is a much-decorated Boer War veteran who never lost his taste for blood. 'Private killing' for him is like 'the fun of shooting big game' but 'The Boer War ... made big game hunting seem as tame as firin' at a few monkeys' (pp. 149–150).

Contemporary feminist critics are beginning to examine the implications of Franklin's politics and gender for her fiction. Rejecting previous readings of her work that focused largely on nationalist questions, critics in recent articles have offered various readings of Franklin as a woman writer: in a women's tradition, in a colonial women's tradition or in an Australian women's tradition, for example.[10] Franklin's feminism is more complex than the evidence of her fiction alone suggests, but, in this case, it is still of interest to see how her feminism has influenced her production of a mystery novel.

In *Bring the Monkey*, the independence of Zarl and the narrator is often measured by their independence as women from men. In common with other Franklin heroines, they are anti-marriage and anti-romance. To the extent that men can't be trusted to be without at best romantic or, at worst, sexual ambitions, the heroines are also anti-men. Zarl never takes any of her many suitors seriously and is ever anxious to avoid the 'mush' of love. 'England is mawkishly damp already. He always wants to go the whole engine!' she says of Jimmy, her aviator suitor who procures Percy for her (p. 40).

Rather than love, these heroines seek platonic friendship with men but their search seems doomed to failure. In these circumstances, their chief loyalties are to each other (and to Percy). Friendships with women are thus presented positively, as an alternative to unequal gender relationships. Contemporary feminists will notice that celibacy is offered here as a permanent, not a temporary solution although modified to some extent by the novel's status as satire. And unlike some recent novels by women, comic or otherwise, heterosexual love is explicitly rejected but the possibility of sexual relations with women is never mentioned.

In this novel, the anti-romantic sentiments are designed primarily to contribute to the satiric effect. But even in a light novel, such ideas are threatening to some readers. As recently as 1982, Colin Roderick wrote that in *Bring the Monkey*, in relation to what he terms Franklin's 'obsessive loathing of the carnal aspect of love . . . It is all right for the housemaid heroine to have a pet monkey cuddle up to her "bosom" in bed; but it wouldn't do to have bone of her bone and flesh of her flesh in the same position.'[11] It is unclear here whether Roderick refers to husbands or babies. What is clear is that Franklin's satirizing of the conventions of romantic fiction, together with marriage and childbirth, has escaped his attention. More importantly, his comments suggest that anti-feminist attitudes still run deep in some sections of contemporary society. They also suggest that Franklin's literary and political activities merit further attention, albeit of a different kind.

In the meantime, here is *Bring the Monkey*, out of print now for more than fifty years. It was written not long before Franklin returned to Australia to look after her ageing mother. There were still many years of literary work ahead of her. From England she sent her mother some photographs of herself, in a cocktail dress and long gloves, with Peter the monkey. Unlike the houseparty invitation which insists that Zarl bring the monkey with her, Susannah Franklin wrote that she liked the photographs but informed her daughter, 'I wouldn't want to have anything more tangible of the little beast. *Don't bring him here.*'[12]

Bronwen Levy
English Department
University of Queensland

NOTES

1. Quoted in Valerie Kent, 'Alias Miles Franklin' in *Gender, Politics and Fiction: Twentieth Century Australian Women's Novels*, ed. Carole Ferrier (St Lucia: University of Queensland Press, forthcoming).

2. Letter from Miles Franklin to Francis Arthur Jones, 24 July 1933, Miles Franklin Papers, MSS 364, Vol. 81, No. 197, Mitchell Library, Sydney.

3. For further information about the Endeavour Press, see Craig Munro, *Wild Man of Letters: The Story of P.R. Stephensen* (Carlton: Melbourne University Press, 1984), Ch. 8.

4. Letter from Miles Franklin to Francis Arthur Jones, 24 July 1933, Miles Franklin Papers, MSS 364, Vol. 81, No. 197, Mitchell Library, Sydney.

5. Nettie Palmer, 'A Reader's Notebook' in *All About Books*, 10 June, 1933, 87 and 4 December, 1933, 207.

6. Marjorie Barnard, *Miles Franklin* (Melbourne: Hill of Content, 1967), 106.

7. See Dianne Kirkby, 'Miles Franklin on Dearborn Street, Chicago, 1906–15', *Australian Literary Studies*, 10, No. 3 (1982), 344–57.

8. See Barnard, *Miles Franklin* and Kirby, 'Miles Franklin on Dearborn Street'. Also see Verna Coleman, *Her Unknown Brilliant Career: Miles Franklin in America* (London and Sydney: Angus and Robertson, 1981); Drusilla Modjeska, *Exiles at Home: Australian Women Writers 1925–1945* (London and Sydney: Sirius, 1981), Ch. 7; Craig Munro, 'Australia First Women Last: Pro-

Fascism and Anti-Feminism in the 1930s', *Hecate*, 9, 1 & 2 (1983), 25–34; Cassandra Pybus, 'The Real Miles Franklin?', *Meanjin*, 42, No. 4 (1983), 459–68; Jill Roe, 'The Significant Silence: Miles Franklin's Middle Years', *Meanjin*, 39, No. 1 (1980), 48–59.

9. Winifred Stephensen, Diary, 16 July 1932 and 17 July 1932, Box K 164722, Stephensen Papers, Mitchell Library, Sydney.

10. See Frances McInherny, 'Miles Franklin, My Brilliant Career, and the Female Tradition' in *Who is She? Images of Woman in Australian Fiction*, ed. Shirley Walker (St Lucia: University of Queensland Press, 1983), 71–83; Susan Gardner, 'My Brilliant Career: Portrait of the Artist as a "Wild Colonial Girl" in *Gender, Politics and Fiction: Twentieth Century Australian Women's Novels*, ed. Carole Ferrier (University of Queensland Press, forthcoming); Delys Bird, 'Towards an Aesthetics of Australian Women's Fiction: *My Brilliant Career* and *The Getting of Wisdom*', *Australian Literary Studies*, 11, No. 2 (1983), 171–81.

11. Colin Roderick, *Miles Franklin: Her Brilliant Career* (Adelaide: Rigby, 1982), 142.

12. Quoted in Roderick, *Miles Franklin*, 144.

CHAPTER 1

I have always loathed murder.

Once I took not the slightest interest in murder cases. I never read even the most luridly headlined nor the socially shocking. However, the Tattingwood case assaulted my interest, and has forced me to wonder how many other women or men may have killed someone, and escaped detection, or even suspicion: or alternatively, how many may have been wrongfully suspected, accused, or even convicted of murder.

But I loathe murder more than ever, as revolting, stupid, bestial, unnecessary.

To employ Zarl Osterley's locution, it carries a fiendish thing altogether too far.

CHAPTER 2

It all happened through Zarl Osterley's monkey, Percy Macacus Rhesus y Osterley. Until Zarl took the notion to acquire him I had as little interest in monkeys as in murder. There are no monkeys in my native land, except in Zoos, and these had always seemed to me as too repellently like depraved editions of ourselves. Their mournful mien depressed me. But one day when Zarl was restless through being baulked of an Everest expedition, she said 'Let's have a monkey!'

'Where would you keep the brute?' I inquired perfunctorily.

'Here, of course! With us!'

Zarl occupied a flat in a studio building in St John's Wood, London, and I spent much time with her.

'A wart hog would be ever so much more convenient and beautiful,' I responded, continuing to read Julian Huxley.

'But I thought you loved animals?!!!'

'All but monkeys: and I don't love any animals in the bread crock, and on the pillows, as they must be in these town places. Animals and cleanliness can't be together in a flat!'

'But we could train a monkey to do anything.'

'You'd have to hire someone to look after the beast.'

This seemed final. We were in such low water that we could not even hire a char.

No more was said on the subject for a week, then Zarl remarked 'I had an offer of a monkey to-day: he was a bit too big, but lovely. I'll never rest now till I have one.'

I turned and looked at her – this time over a book by Osbert Sitwell. Zarl resembles a champagne glass, not alone

2

in grace of fashioning, but in effervescent contents. The bubbles are intensely fascinating. 'Surely you are not in earnest about a monkey?'

'I must have something. This is dreadful – just going to bed and getting up again – without seeing the sun rise on Kangchenjunga, or the ice break on the Lena.'

'I should have thought you had enough of the sleet on the desolate bays of the Beagle Channel when you went to the Horn.'

'Oh, I've forgotten that long ago. I'm going to concentrate now on going to the Lena or the Indigirka, and I must have a monkey to keep me from doddering into a complete stodge.'

'A monkey would hasten that,' I contended. 'You've seen those old women with poodles – can't tell the women from the poodles – pathetic derelicts – ugh! A monkey would do that for you – only more so.'

'A monkey would be a symbol and a promise.'

'A sure promise of wrecking everything in the place, and think of the SMELL!!!'

'I never heard that monkeys *smell*!'

'Then you must have been very deaf in the Zoo.'

'But I'd only have one.'

I had visions of Zarl's establishment degenerating into a kennel. Zarl is not a Martha among housewives. That is one of her great charms; one can live with her without ceaseless petty persecution. A London interior becomes sufficiently trying with a cat or dog – but a monkey! Good-bye to our pleasant association. I comforted myself by thinking that the monkey would never materialise.

But a week later Zarl came bubbling in. 'I've got a monkey!'

'Where? How? What!'

'Jimmy Wengham brought five back in an aeroplane from Africa, but only one has lived, and he has kept it for me. Someone has it somewhere, and I'm going there to get it. It will be too marvellously thrilling. "Wizard! Eh, what?" as Jimmy says.'

I took a farewell glance around the fine room with its comfortable chairs, reflected that all things bright and fair are fleeting, and retreated to my own lair. But next day, as I was descending, Zarl was ascending my stairs.

'Look! I thought you'd like to see Percy – my monkey. I've had a terrible time with him. He's bitten me, and I could never confess how many things he has broken. I don't think he has been kindly treated. He has a great scar on his leg – poor little cow.'

I beheld a creature the size of a half-grown kitten, only more slender, an appealing, shrinking mite that tried to creep out of sight under Zarl's furs. He shuddered and showed his teeth in a piteous grin, as if I were a big baboon that would demolish him. I can never resist any animal, even the so-called human ones, if they appear distressful, and I took this poor little soul in my arms and attempted to stroke his fur, but he shivered through every fibre at the slightest touch, and looked so woebegone that I was instantaneously and permanently enslaved.

'He's behaving very well with you,' remarked Zarl. 'Would you like to keep him all night? I've got a chance to be motored up to Cambridge for the week-end, and there is a professor there who might like to go down the Lena to the Arctic Sea for the goose-plucking, and to see that thinga-me-bob bird; and Percy might get in the way at the wrong moment.'

I was committed to Percy for one night, for two, for three. We were left to make acquaintance as best we would. I washed all his human hands and face, and he enjoyed dabbling in the warm water and grabbing the soap. I made him clean and sweet, settled the matter of loin cloths after the fashion of Mahatma Gandhi, gave him a cup of milk to hold in his own tiny hands, got him a blanket and box, tethered him to the leg of my bed, and retired.

I peeped up now and again to see if he were there, to savour the delight of such a guest. And every time I peeped, he would be peeping too, to see what I intended. It was so amusing that I laughed aloud, cheered and entertained. Never since my teens, in the joy of new kittens, or a baby koala, or an echidna, had I felt such pleasure.

In the morning he came to bed to be cuddled, a warm delicately-fashioned little thing of sensitive texture. How ignorant I had been to think of a monkey only as ugly or evil-smelling! Here were beauty and grace to nourish the aesthetic appetite.

In the days that followed, Percy settled in. I had been thoroughly grounded by my mother in the ethics of pets. She always said, 'Unless you are willing to do *everything* for either a child or an animal, you do not *really* love it; you only love yourself and the sensuous pleasure to be derived from it.' The world is full of the less thorough kind of lovers. There is little competition on the other plane, so Percy quickly developed into a personality, with me as a coolie on the end of his string. A flatette was vacated in Zarl's building and I moved there to be near him. We devoted ourselves to making him happy, and to surrounding him with that affection said to be necessary for the flowering of a monkey's genius. This was due to one exiled from his own sunny country to make a toy for people who should have known better. He devoured as much time as cross-word puzzles or bridge – more than we could afford – and was an expensive luxury for hard-working women; but in an age of people rendered superfluous by machines, the teeth were drawn from the rebuke that we would have been better employed as mothers dragging-up infants to degenerate in uselessness.

Fulminations against a mischievous, unfaithful, trouble-some invention of sheer pestiferation collapsed. Percy had only to dance before us, or to hold out a confiding hand, to break loose and jump into bed with us, or cry if we left him alone, and our hearts were softened.

In the way of sirens of either sex and of any size or shape he was irresistible – a continual nuisance and a perpetual delight. He was a 'wow' in several sets, a favourite in the Parks and on many 'buses and in the Underground. To his popularity and my infatuation can be attributed my connec-tion with what is here recorded.

CHAPTER 3

Through the evidence and gossip that surrounded the case, by information gleaned from an articulate police official, by deduction and inference – without which any chronicler is a dunce – there was no difficulty in reconstructing the procedure preliminary to Lady Tattingwood's party.

The impending week-end at Tattingwood Hall was noted by the Yard. After the years of comparative freedom from robberies upon jewel owners, which had followed the smashing of Cammi Grizard's and Leiser Guttwirth's gangs just before the war, there had been recently a recrudescence of such depredations. It looked as if the lesser gangs which had been disrupted in the late twenties, by the arrest and conviction of the master spirits, were attempting re-organisation around new leaders.

The tactics of Ydonea Zaltuffrie, the dazzling film star, were such as to generate independent burglarious activities. Her press agent's concoctions raved through the press with such virulence that the police had had to disperse the traffic outside the Ritz. The credulous were doped by the news that she was so startlingly beautiful that she ravaged the hearts of princes and rajahs, as well as those of talking-picture fanatics. She was now about to lay waste the remnants of the English aristocracy. She was to open her campaign in one of the few remaining country houses, where the Hon. Cedd Ingwald Swithwulf Spillbeans, second son of the family, had taken to films as a career. They allured him as a more pulsating adventure than that followed by his elder brother St. Erconwald, in securing, without any thrills or frills, a nice tame heiress, who had risen to the demands of primogeniture by producing two male infants.

Owing to post-war taxes and the rising cost of living in every direction, the Baron himself was threadbare. Tattingwood Hall had become a devouring monster that put him on the rack. Keep it up as of yore, he could not; give it up he would not – not even to his son to evade death duties. It was his life, his love, his religion, his hobby. His second wife had been chosen for the sake of Tattingwood – a Miss Clarice Lesserman. (Soap.) She had invested in Lord Tattingwood some ten years before I met her, for the glamour of the title, and as a bulwark against a war-time infatuation for a man many years her junior. Now mergers, rationalisation and other humorosities of business efficiency were deflating her suds and paralysing her products far below the needs of Tattingwood Hall.

She had no declared children of her own, so was comfortably assimilated by her step-sons, and she welcomed the distractions of the younger's film enterprises.

This week-end was the apex of opportunity towards which Cedd had been diligently working for months. To have captured the fabulous Ydonea Zaltuffrie, in itself was achievement, and the idea was to involve her to the extent of starring in a film story which Cedd had gathered together without the interference of an author. Cedd hoped to direct it. He was even prepared to marry Ydonea for a spell, should art or career demand such lengths. That she might be too independent to marry him, he was not quite Over-Seas or post-war enough to grasp.

Lady Tattingwood had become friends with Zarl Osterley on Mount Cook or Lake Taupo, where she had gone to get a little fresh air, being that way inclined, and where Zarl had lent her some safety-pins in emergency. Lady Tattingwood had been there for fresh air, it has been suggested, and Zarl was taking a little exercise, because one of her fortes is to be secretary to some great man or another on hegiras to the ends of the earth to meditate upon the past history or to inspect the present private life of some bug or weed. This gave her an intimate nook in many different cliques.

Lady Tattingwood was uneasy about the Ali Baba trove of

jewels advertised in connection with her film star guest, who wore them with a nonchalance becoming to beads from Woolworth's. There was no telling whom they might attract to the village, so Lady Tattingwood had a heart-to-heart talk with the local police. Lord Tattingwood sent a peremptory message to New Scotland Yard. This was considered by the right official and passed on to Chief Inspector Stopworth. The Yard had earlier been consulted by Miss Zaltuffrie's Grand Vizier, with the result that a Yard officer was to reinforce the lady's private detective force.

The Chief Inspector, or Captain Stopworth, as he was more familiarly known to his friends, considered the police aspects of Miss Zaltuffrie's advent. Her pictures met him on every illustrated page, and some of them were remarkable. It was not her beauty however, but her jewels that interested Captain Stopworth. It was rumoured that the heir to the Maharajah of Bong or Bogwallah, or some such marvellous or mythical principality, had gone mad about Ydonea in Paris. The press freely stated that he had given her stupendous State Jewels, but probably there was exaggeration in the interests of a commercial headline or two.

Captain Stopworth had plenty of salt to sprinkle on such 'publicity,' to keep down mortification, but he carefully extracted the grains of news, and re-read Lord Tattingwood's demand. He then put through a call to Supersnoring and requested the Butler to bring Lady Tattingwood to the telephone. When he had established his identity, the Inspector asked her ladyship to inform her husband that there would be a sergeant and constable in his service from Saturday night till Monday morning; and then his tone changed.

'I have not seen you for a long time, old girl.'

'Whose fault is that?'

'Well, have you a spare bed for this week-end? I could kill two birds – from Saturday afternoon till Sunday after dinner.'

'Yes, oh, my dear, do come, and bring what we spoke of. It will be safe. I'll explain when you are here.'

'All right. I'll see you some time during the next forty-eight hours – privately I mean: *au revoir*.'

He replaced the instrument and tattooed a tune on his desk for a few moments while sunk in thought. He then touched a buzzer and a smart young officer came in. Calls to the Ritz Hotel and the Mayfair Police Station were then put through, and there were conferences. Eventually Captain Stopworth informed Detective-Constable Manning that he would proceed to Tattingwood Hall for the week-end in the role of valet, while Detective-Sergeant Beeton was to have the privilege of being present to see Cedd Spillbeans' film, he supposedly being interested in sport and the allied arts.

CHAPTER 4

'It's getting to be a pretty pass with me to be invited for that!' exclaimed Zarl with humorous petulance as she stood before the long mirror and arranged a delectable copper-tinted curl on her forehead. She refers to herself as ginger, but that is affectation. Her hair is that incredible shade that shames a new penny, and challenges armour. It matches the little dancing flecks in her soft round eyes.

She tossed a letter on stationery embossed TATTINGWOOD HALL, SUPERSNORING, with a telephone exchange in the Home Counties.

> My darling Zarl,
>   Do come for the week-end, and bring the Monkey. Ydonea Zaltuffrie is to be here, and if Cedd's machinations hang fire, what am I to do with such a white elephant? She is dripping in beauty and 'it' and dresses mostly in jewels, given her by some Indian Prince whose name is never mentioned for fear of making things worse in India. So Swithwulf has dubbed him the Rajah of Bogwallah for convenience. Do bring the monkey. This is a genuine S.O.S. Besides, I'm dying to make his acquaintance. Swithwulf has called in Scotland Yard because of the jewels. Jimmy Wengham is to be here too. Don't fail me.
>
>   Clarice.

'Did you *ever*! I must be degenerating into a sorry old tart – like an organ-grinder invited to bringa-da-monk to entertain a flicker doll with goggle eyes, who registers the lowest paroxysms of osculation as a substitute for witchery every time some Buffalo Bill whiffles through a megaphone.'

'I shouldn't mind being considered a tart with a tom cat, or I'd even be civil to one of those goggle-eyed frowsy Pekes to gain admittance to so marvellous a menagerie. I begrudge Percy Macacus Rhesus y Osterley, he is all that has stood between me and jumping-off this last week.'

I was spread in a deep chair, my feet to the fire with Percy on my chest under my oldest woolly jersey, fast asleep. The lovable face showed complete abandon, the closed eyelids were an eggshell blue that left those of the painted ladies mere 'mucky pups.'

'You come, too. I'll wire Clarice. She'll be delighted. She's a kind old pillow.'

'I've just refused the party at Buckhurst because I cannot afford the tips in those private pubs – prefer the regular inns; besides, I've only got one evening gown spry enough.'

'I haven't a stitch either; and imagine me in evening dress with Percy! He'd pluck every feather off me, and leave bleeding weals on my most important promontories. The odious little cow never cares a hoot about the side his bread is buttered, and favours all the wrong people. He'll most likely go for old Swith's nose.'

'He evidently knows how to annex a faithful coolie,' I said, tilting his chin the better to adore him. He made little guffing sounds of protest against being disturbed, and crawled farther under my jersey.

'He really *is* consistent about you. It makes me think he must have some character or intellect. If you won't come with me, come with Percy to Tattingwood Hall.'

'I've got an idea! I'll go as your maid in overalls, to take care of Percy. I shall be saved from the woofits, and you'll help Lady Tattingwood to offset Ydonea. My new dress will be free for your use too.'

'Don't be a peanut! What an entertaining but utterly impossible idea – some one there might know you.'

'No. When I ascend to society, it is to a much more political sociological clique who do good to humanity; also I'll be disguised in a uniform. Who ever looks at a maid at one of those jamborees – plenty of hunting higher up. If I wanted to commit a crime, I'd take Percy, and then everyone would be looking at him and fail to see me. Yes, let's rival Ydonea!'

'Why should I waste my fleeting moments on the oddments that infest Clarice – not one of them could be excited to go as far as the Murrumbidgee, let alone the Indigirka or Lena.'

'What about Jimmy Wengham? I see in the papers that he is the pilot of Ydonea's aircraft – going to fly to glory. I should think he might be useful for your expedition.'

'Aaaahhhh! Has she swallowed Jimmy? I might induce regurgitation, just to see.'

We telephoned a telegram:

DELIGHTED BRINGING MONKEY AND MAID SATURDAY FOUR O'CLOCK ZARL

We were in the midst of our preparations when Lady Tattingwood's reply came:

AFRAID NO ROOM FOR MAID HOUSE FULL SORRY LOVE CLARICE

'Well then, it's off, and I contribute Jimmy to Ydonea's bag,' said Zarl. 'And I'm glad, as I'd much rather do something quietly with you. Please send another telegram.'

Unselfishness is one of the prominent ingredients of Zarl's seductiveness. She was obviously planning to keep me from melancholia during the weekend, because I had lately been knocked into a cocked hat, but I did not want to burden her unduly. I went to the telephone and sent another message:

MAID THOROUGHLY RESPECTABLE GIVE HER MATTRESS IN MY ROOM NECESSARY FOR MONKEY ZARL

'There, you must live up to me now. Percy will be an opening for me to be in the whole shoot, above stairs and below – a two-ring comedy.'

I hauled Percy from a picture, where he was investigating an electric wire, and lashed him to a divan leg, where he

began to shred the valance with perfect good-will and
gentlemanliness.

CHAPTER 5

It was a clammy day towards the end of the year with enough roke to close it early, and a good many of the guests were assembled in the great hall when Zarl entered a few minutes past four o'clock. We had arrived at Supersnoring by train, where Lady Tattingwood's motor was awaiting us and two other unclassified guests. Zarl attended to our suitcases while I nursed Percy. His weight was six pounds but his energy made it seem like fifteen, and his resourcefulness and perseverance in employing it were an object lesson to the discouraged. And he can reach as far – well, he can simply reach, and reach, and reach till he gets there. Zarl had to be protected from him till the right moment, or she might arrive with the air of one of those frumps in employment agencies waiting for jobs that always pass them by. I was provided with overalls and a bag of tricks such as a mother takes abroad with a young infant. Percy's wardrobe was extensive.

It is worth going to Tattingwood in any capacity to see the lovely old place crowning the Park as one approaches by the long, sunken drive. To halt under the arch of the tower and turn to the left up the imposing steps that lead to the big chamber called 'the hall' is sheer adventure. The noble beauty of these old places goes to my head.

At the right moment Zarl tucked Percy under her arm with a Judo clasp, that has proved successful, and made an effective entrance. Percy was the right shade to go with her trim coat and skirt, and peeped most endearingly from her fabulous furs, that came straight from Alaska or some such place. I was alert lest he should destroy them; on another occasion

14

he had chewed the head off a mink stole while Zarl was engaged in conversation. He had been too good to be harmless.

Lady Tattingwood, a colourless but unmistakably kind looking woman, like a patroness of suburban charities or the Women's Institutes, welcomed us all three with eager cordiality, and drew us towards one of the two great fires with which the hall was enlivened. Percy creates a diversion in any society, so interesting are animals, but he was a godsend to a company that needed dancing, bridge, gramophone, radio, billiards or something like that to make up for the dearth of inner resources all the time that *amour* was not on draft.

An elephant hunter from the Congo was presented to Zarl, and with him was Jimmy Wengham, late R.A.F. I pulled my cap lower lest Jimmy may have remembered seeing me at Zarl's one evening. He was an exceedingly tall dark dissipated-looking young man, and had a name for general as well as aerial recklessness. He had retreated from the Air Force because he had used one of the Government planes for his own excursions.

He and the Elephant Hunter had been engaged in throwing knives into a board set up as a target across a corner. Jimmy informed Zarl that the Elephant Hunter was at present in the lead, as he had the more patience. The Elephant Hunter was another very tall man, by name, Brodribb, stolid and with eyes of elephant grey – protective colouration perhaps – which may have been excellent for sighting big game, but had a disconcertingly static stare for a house party.

Lord Tattingwood entered with a curious weapon about the size of a dirk, but more the shape of a rapier, as though a rapier with a small hilt had been cut down to nine or twelve inches, and filed very sharp.

He greeted Zarl, and poked his finger under Percy's neck, causing him to shudder and click irascibly. He said facetiously 'Shall I do the little blighter in with this – it wouldn't be the first of his species. Seen dozens like him cut up to flavour the Zulus' soup in South Africa.'

The knife throwers were tremendously interested in their host's unconventional weapon, which he said he had had since the Boer war. Both men immediately tried it on the board. Wengham was fascinated by the sport of throwing it to strike into the wood.

'By George! It could be a dangerous thing!' he exclaimed.

'It used to be when I was your age,' admitted his host.

He was urged to try his skill now, but after wavering and twisting, the knife fell short from his hand and made a hole in one of the great rugs. 'I've lost my nerve and judgment of distance,' he said, turning to talk to Zarl. She left the young men to their sport, as we both have a horror of knives. Jimmy Wengham took no notice of Percy. He was engrossed in the new sport and had not a capacious mind. He had not given me a glance fortunately. Lord Tattingwood, on the contrary, fixed me with a steadfast glare.

Nothing but his height fitted the figure of Swithwulf George Cedd St. Erconwald Spillbeans to be the sixteenth Baron Tattingwood and Lord of that splendid pile. He was stooping, shabby and dull – a dowdy old man in the sixties. Disappointing. Zarl went the rounds, while I, thanks to Percy, stood by the door enjoying the promising comedy.

Ydonea Zaltuffrie was not in evidence. A number of the other women guests had also disappeared to put on something startling for the tea hour, which was approaching. Lady Tattingwood, placing her arm around Zarl affectionately, and again thanking her for coming and bringing 'the dear little monkey,' said she would go upstairs with her. In ordinary circumstances I should have been drafted off to the lower regions, but Zarl transferred the monkey to my arms and said 'Come along with him now.'

'Yes,' confirmed Lady Tattingwood, 'Come with us now.'

We ascended the grand main staircase and turned to the left. Lady Tattingwood's apartments were in a corner which faced the Park on one side. We were put into a large room adjoining. It had been occupied by Lord Tattingwood during his first marriage, but he now occupied a suite in the east wing. There was rather a large bed, and, placed at the foot of it, was a stretcher. Zarl's quarters were a *ménage à trois* by reason of Percy and me. Lady Tattingwood apologised that she had had to give the dressing-room on the other side to Captain Stopworth at the last moment.

16

'I am so sorry to have turned him out,' said Zarl, 'But you brought it on yourself.'

'It is he who has cramped your quarters,' she replied. 'But with the Maharajah's jewels plastered on Miss Zaltuffrie, instead of an idol that could be locked up, I had to have protection. Such a relief to turn the supervision of safety over to Captain Stopworth. It leaves me free to help Cedd with his film fortunes.'

Zarl chaffed her friend in low tones; and discussed Jimmy Wengham. When he had crashed out of his Commission in the R.A.F. owing to the abduction of a sacred war machine for a commercial stunt, Jimmy had distinguished himself by one of the first flights to South Africa in company with a titled air woman, who became desperately enamoured of him. Jimmy however was infatuated with Zarl at that date, to the extent of lugging home a family of monkeys. His present idea was to stunt in films and thus collect funds for a record world flight. He had quite smartly got himself elected as pilot of Ydonea's new Puss Moth and was spreading himself as a prominent member of the star's retinue. Ydonea had her eye on his publicity possibilities and for the moment tolerated his standardised amorous cacklings.

While Zarl and her hostess talked, I opened the suitcases and made pretentious play for my mistress *pro tem*, by laying out the gorgeous pyjamas which were reserved for show and creating envy. Also laid out for her was my one smart new evening gown.

'Don't leave any of the windows open on to the terraces,' warned Clarice. 'We must guard against entrances for suspicious characters that may be attracted by the jewels.'

'It is too thrilling for reality to have the famous Capt. Stopworth right next door to us,' said Zarl.

'Hurry down and help us through tea,' said her hostess. 'And bring Percy, too. Dear wee creature, I am so proud that he has come to spend a week-end with me, and hope he will be happy.'

'*He* will be, but I don't know about you, by the time you'll be finished with him,' laughed Zarl.

As soon as Clarice left us we moored Percy to the big coal scuttle into which we piled a door weight and other

17

unchewable articles. The scuttle was put in a clear space near the foot of the bed and Percy given a short leash. In his search for insects and the establishment of hygiene, which was a major business with the little fellow, we hoped he would not pull the pattern out of the carpet, or reach and reach in his elastic capacity till he shredded the bed clothes or pulled over the dressing table.

I plastered myself with a brunette cosmetic that made me resemble an American Indian. Over a brown gown I wore a smart orange apron, and around my short crisp locks wrapped an orange bandeau to match the apron. 'An accent will heighten your importance,' I said to Zarl. My sporting instinct stirred to outplay Ydonea Zaltuffrie's maid, no matter what she might be.

'Don't be too ambitious, or I may crack in trying to live up to you.'

Zarl had an arresting suit of lounge pyjamas for tea, in electric light exactly the colour of her hair. It had been lent to us out of stock for this prank by our friend Mabelle. (Madame Mabelle, Exclusive Gowns, Loane Street, Knightsbridge, where Zarl at that time had a post).

Zarl was to depend upon the monkey for distinctive *decor*. We couldn't risk his chewing up a forty guinea garment, which was worth at least fifteen guineas on its merits, and Percy quite innocently could leave disreputable hieroglyphs on bosom or cheek, as he struggled towards one for refuge. Therefore where the monkey was, I had to be also, a gilt-edged scheme to be in all the fun without the burden of being entertaining, or having to appear in evening uniform, like a plucked fowl in an ice box; and so inexpensive, compared with being a guest.

Percy had the most adorable little knitted singlet and brown velvet shorts, and sported a strong new lead. All his four hands were cleanly washed in warm water and scented soap, and his nose was powdered. He loved to participate in Zarl's toilette secrets, which were very simple, and no secrets at all. The entertaining little beggar added just the requisite touch of unusuality to Zarl, who generally conquered the wariest by her natural delight in the passing hour. She was stimulated by the prospect of Ydonea, and went down the stairs with a mischievous champagne-bubble expression in her eyes, and the lights making mocking fires in her curls.

CHAPTER 6

Her entry was not to be jeopardised by precipitancy, and while we had been waiting she informed me that during the war, Tattingwood Hall had been lent as a hospital for officers, and Clarice Lesserman had worked there as a V.A.D. Thus had she met her future husband, and also a handsome young second lieutenant, Cecil Stopworth. Away out on the shores of Lake Taupo, Lady Tattingwood had told some of her story to Zarl — the more romantic parts, her tongue loosened to sentimental reminiscence by the inebriating New Zealand moonlight. Lady Tattingwood's friends — so-called — had told Zarl other facets of the affair later.

Glamorous days for Clarice, aging and disillusioned, to look back upon, days when she had nearly run away with the handsome boy, son of an impoverished Indian Civil Servant, whose University career had been interrupted to join up. She had been saved on the brink of folly because whispering tongues insisted upon the fact that she was twelve years her lover's senior, and rich, very rich, and the war was making her much richer, while he would have to depend on his own exertions. Some people, who meant well, put old Lesserman on the trail. Others had suggested that Stopworth was a caddish fortune hunter. In the antipodean moonlight Clarice confessed to Zarl her regrets that she had not risked all, because Cecil Stopworth's name had never from that day onward been connected with other women. His affection might have been that one example in a million of lasting romance, despite disparity in age and fortune.

The not very serious wounds that had taken Stopworth to

20

Tattingwood Military Hospital, were all that he suffered in the war. He rose to be a Captain, won the Military Cross, and in due order was demobilised and thrown on his own resources. To return to the University was impossible. He had not the means, and had lost the urge. His father had died and his mother was reduced to a small pension. He had the experience of many other young men following the war, and in desperation filed an application, and was accepted as a member of the Police Force.

He had been too proud to permit Clarice Lesserman to sacrifice herself by eloping with him.

In the Force he found work that he liked, and when practicable made application for removal to the Criminal Investigation Department, where he quickly attracted attention. His rise was rapid owing to his successful solution of several criminal mysteries. He came of a good family, and, as the years passed, he renewed his acquaintance with Lady Tattingwood. As he had simple tastes and remained a bachelor, his salary was sufficient for his needs, and he was sometimes to be seen at other week-ends too. It was predicted that he would one day be Commissioner. He was well-suited to his post and seemed to have no interests outside it. With his splendid good looks, charming manners and ability he could easily have advanced himself by marriage, but women were not one of his weaknesses. No one believed that he had a throb of anything but friendship for Clarice, because she looked her years without subterfuge, but the lamp that she had lighted for him was still burning. She was fortunate beyond the dreams of most women that he never humiliated her by affairs with other women, at least none that were known to her circle.

She was now fifty-one or -two, and Captain Stopworth in the last of his thirties. I was glad that the hero of this interesting romance was to be quartered almost with us.

There had been no romance in the second marriage of Tattingwood to Clarice Lesserman. Everyone knew it for what it was. The lady, when forty, had contributed her fortune to the support of Tattingwood Hall in return for position and name. It served as well as most unions, and was a splendid investment for many of those who depended on week-ends. Tattingwood liked to dispense hospitality in the pre-war way, and Clarice was so kind and unforceful that she never made anyone unhappy.

Zarl assured me that Lord Tattingwood had not always been the frump of to-day. His life had been full of romance. His father was only second cousin of the Fifteenth Baron, and Swithwulf had been designed for the Church. He had escaped this for the army, and had his chance in the Boer war, from which he returned a hero with the V.C. He had been invited by his elderly cousin to stay with the son and heir, a quiet soul addicted to the laboratory, and with no taste for being a landed gentleman. He looked forward with regret to stepping into his father's shoes, whereas Swithwulf would have sold his soul to possess the old place. It was a passion with him. A great horseman, a crack shot, a champion at games, he was a popular figure. People said it was a pity that he could not change with the heir, to whom hunting and similar pursuits were a burden. When it happened that the young man accidentally shot himself and Swithwulf reigned in his stead, all seemed as it should have been.

My head was full of the story as I went down to tea in the wake of Zarl with Percy in my arms. We could not allow him to be near the lounge suite. He had had a good snooze in the train and was far from a cuddly mood, alert to leap in all directions like a crab propelled by a jennie wink. He was so beyond reason that I put him down, whereupon he descended the stairs with dignity. He liked Tattingwood Hall as much as I did, and probably for analogous reasons. Its spaciousness suggested our native habitats. He slid forward utterly silent, with an electric ease approaching that of fish in water. Arrived amid the company, all eyes were his, as always, wherever he appeared in whatever society.

Zarl's status was quite well upheld by her maid's smart uniform, and, with the addition of Percy, it would be difficult for any other maid to be more special. Zarl was so bewitching in her modish garments and astonishing curls that it would take a transcendant film star to eclipse her.

Cedd Spillbeans came towards her. 'Hello! Why this organ-grinder monkey motley touch?'

'I'm so broke that I hope you'll cross Percy's hand with silver.'

At this, Jimmy Wengham, who was still practising with the dirk in the corner, desisted, and exclaimed 'Surely that's not the stinkin' little blighter I brought over in the old Haviland.'

'No one ever knew Zarl so long faithful to any male,' said young Spillbeans.

'Do you mean the monkey or me?' demanded Wengham.

On beholding the company, Percy bolted to my arms and showed his teeth in a grin that was merely nervous, but which to the uninitiated looked vicious. One affected lady of mature years, in the dress of a flapper, made a fuss of 'the dear little darling' and wanted to clasp him to her attenuated frame, but the monkey is not that kind of cat. Percy threw himself about and attempted to smack the lady.

'Spiteful little creature,' she hissed, and turned to the company. 'Monkeys are dangerous things. You *never* can trust them, *Never*! I know of awful cases of accidents with them. He's just a *common* little monkey, isn't he?'

'I wish the little cow would understand which side his bread is buttered,' whispered Zarl to me.

'He's going to, this evening,' I whispered in return.

He was not at all attracted to the company filling the hall. He clutched me tight and tried to climb inside my dress. At the approach of Wengham he screeched and fluffed out his fur and became a fierce beast in miniature.

'Ha! Ha! Jimmy,' exclaimed Zarl. 'What did you do to him when you were travelling together?'

Everyone laughed, to the discomfiture of Jimmy. 'I had to keep the little blighters in order. You're only a little mongrel, not worth the trouble you were,' he said, tickling Percy under the chin. 'Say Zarl, will you let me take a shot at him at twenty paces with this knife. Just for practice!'

'He notta like you,' I murmured, gathering Percy to me.

'The little fellow feels instinctively that you are one of those horrid blood sports creatures,' said Zarl.

He settled down somewhat, but peeped entertainingly at his enemy, raising his fur. To divert him I set him before a long mirror, and much to the glee of the company he danced for the fellow monkey that he saw in its depths.

'Say Zarl,' called Jimmy, 'Don't you want to come with me on a world flight, and bring the monkey for a mascot? It would be simply coloss!'

'It would be *colossal*! When do we start?' demanded Zarl, the champagne bubbles rising, and her sudden interest in Jimmy going to his head.

'Just as soon as I gather the beans. If you and the monkey could charm some fat-necked millionaire into providing a machine – a Puss Moth like Miss Zaltuffrie's.'

'What is the matter with Miss Zaltuffrie's?'

'Now that's a wizard idea! I've got everything wrapped-up except money. The thing is to get away ahead of the crowd! It's a damned pity you aren't an heiress, Zarl!'

'I find it an inconvenience myself, but the inevitable fate of heiresses consoles me.' She could have been thinking of her hostess as her host shambled about.

'The competition is awful when the heiress isn't,' admitted Jimmy, 'but I must get money somewhere, even if I turn burglar.'

'Your state of mind should be reported to Captain Stop-worth,' said Zarl, as a gentleman entered from the stairway. He came straight to Percy. So this was the famous Chief Inspector! He had the touch that goes with love of animals. Percy looked steadily up at him from his pretty brown eyes so beautifully set in the dearest of little faces, and offered a tiny hand. He took the Captain's thumb in his mouth, and next tried to chew a button off his coat.

'What a success he would be on the films,' the Inspector remarked, and strolled over to help his hostess with the placing of the tea trays. Her eyes lighted at his approach. It would be much more difficult to be sure of the state of the handsome Captain's emotions.

'What should be reported to me?' he inquired lightly.

'Only that Jimmy says he would do anything for money, and so should I, if I had an easy chance.'

'Go on the films,' recommended the gentleman.

'It would be as easy to win the Hospital Sweep,' said Zarl.

The tea was cooling as the air grew heavier with the imminence of Ydonea Zaltuffrie. All the social members of her retinue were suitably disposed about the interior, among

24

them, her mother, a plain woman from the Middle-West who stuck to her plain name of Mrs. Burden. She was called Mrs. Zaltuffrie, but more generally 'Mommer.' Ydonea so patently capitalised the universal mother complex that Mommer Zaltuffrie was suspected of being a hard-fisted and -headed non-relative hired to play the sentimental part. Managers, directors or such potentates of the industry stood about and made standardised pronouncements on the beauty and clever-ness of Miss Zaltuffrie, or emitted spontaneous 'best bets' or 'wise-cracks' as to what would relieve the slump in the trade. One had one dearth of idea, and one another, but they were generally agreed that the total elimination of the author would be a tremendous advance. One little man evidently had a place in the industry as commanding as his proboscis. 'An imposing thing carried altogether too far,' as Zarl described it. It was likewise bearded within, which thickened his accent. 'Not an accent, the honk of a siren, yet not a siren,' again to quote Zarl.

'Authors,' said the gentleman, 'Are the bummest lot of cranks I have ever been up against. Why the heck they aren't content to beat it once they get a price for their stuff, gets my goat.'

'I'll say you've thrown off a mouthful there,' agreed his companion. 'They are egotistical and jealous as cats. What surprises me about them – or it don't surprise me no longer – is that they can't say anything interesting to me.'

There was ready agreement that authors were a wanton tax on any industry, whether publishing, drama or pictures.

'Then why have them at all?' interposed Zarl.

'The public has kinda gotta complex about authors. It's an old sooperstition hard to banish. They think you gotta have a big author; and the bigger they are the deader they are above the neck.'

'They're just the dumbest things,' said another.

'Perhaps if you lent them your megaphones they could be noisier,' suggested Zarl.

'They sure need something,' agreed the honk from the bearded beak. 'You can wear your life away making them known and then they think you are trying to rob them. If you use a few of their little wise cracks . . .'

25

'It might be a colossically new idea to crack your own wisdom,' interpolated Zarl, 'and teach the cows a lesson.' She was so enchantingly demure that Cedd Spillbeans came to the rescue of his guests.

'I understand your point of view,' he said suavely. 'That is why I want you to see my film – one reason. It has been assembled by experts in the industry, not written by some wayward outsider.'

'Oh, Boy! You've said something there. That's what put it across with me.'

'Yeah! Me too! Right away when I asked who was the author and you said you had given those old guys the go by . . .'

The cue for Ydonea's entry interrupted this speaker, a virtuoso with a formidable cigar that lolled upon his lips like a German sausage sustained by miraculous levitation. The million dollar beauty was coming, in the part of enchanted fairy princess. Her aureole of hair was palest gold, commercialised as platinum – still more costly. She was a pioneer in this innovation. It suggested ethereality as she descended with the light from a great glass chandelier upon it. The first sight of such fresh young beauty was breath-taking. Her form was tall and lily slender, but voluptuous – no skinniness – supple as an oriental dancer's. Her nose was perfect in bridge and nostrils, her eye-brows dark, her lashes long. She had one of those mouths so obligingly patterned that she had only to part the bowed lips to make a smile to cheer a photographer. She wore her nails long and claw-like and bright rose. Her eyes matched her mouth and nose in beauty. They were large and meltingly brown – like Percy's. There was no nerviness to give them exotic meaning. Her laughter was not the kind that puts wrinkles at the top of the cheeks, but no one would discern this while such beauty was so loudly advertised, at least no infatuated male creature. A sober woman remarking it would be suspected of envy.

She impersonated perfectly the exquisite unspotted maiden, with Mommer ever at hand as a fortification against fornication and other vulgarities ancient and modern. She was attired with that utter simplicity attainable by none but famous couturiers regardless of expense, and had no jewel or

26

ornament upon her person. No silks or velvets for afternoon tea, but some mythical stuff, like sunkist ivory sea foam against a cliff, frothed down the dark stairs. Her man secretary, a young Englishman with a public school 'mannah,' who had been engaged for decorative purposes, carried her billowing train, while her rousing utilitarian American woman secretary came behind him and kept a managerial eye on the tableau. When Ydonea halted, her mother rose and fluffed out her train around her with a few finishing touches as to a little girl going to a party. These endearments were advertised as too sweet and 'cute for anything in middle-class minded society, but were critically received by the assembled hard-bitten fox-hunters and poor relations.

'Oh, a dear 'cute little monkey!' exclaimed Ydonea, declining tea and coming towards Percy.

Miss Bitcalf-Spillbeans, whom Percy had rebuffed earlier in the evening, hastened to say that monkeys were never safe, *never*. Secretaries and Mommer advised Ydonea to be careful, but she liked the long mirror as much as did Percy, and came on.

Percy had been prepared by a slender diet during twenty-four hours, as he is more amenable with an appetite than with a full tummy. I unostentatiously handed Ydonea a baked chestnut. For this bribe Percy ecstatically deserted me, being that way constituted morally. He sat in Ydonea's arms expertly tearing the hull off the dainty, emitting engaging grunts of satisfaction. Miss Zaltuffrie expressed her delight.

'Oh, boy! I don't know when I've had such a kick out of anything!'

When Percy had finished the chestnut he began to chaw a hole in the diaphanous sleeve of her gown and then to rend it right and left. He loved to tear rag. His new friend would not permit his pleasure to be curtailed. A lady who could command contracts for fifty thousand pounds at par was not obliged to be uneasy about her finery.

'It doesn't matter. He can have the whole thing to play with, the 'cute little darling. I just love him to death right away.'

Miss Zaltuffrie must have a monkey forthwith. She could not understand why she had not thought of one before. 'Why didn't I think of having a monkey?' she demanded of Zarl, who murmured disarmingly that it was easier to let others think.

'I must have one for my next picture. I'll have this one. Whose is he?' she demanded of me. I indicated Zarl, who was sitting on a pouff on the hearth rug smoking one of the Elephant Hunter's cigarettes, while Jimmy Wengham gazed down at her with a he-man craving inflaming his expression.

Ydonea again turned in that direction, clicking her fingers to draw attention. 'Say, Miss, on the Turkish cushion, what do you want for your monkey?'

Zarl, if she heard, affected not to. She continued her jocular blandishments.

'Say, Miss Zaltuffrie is wanting you,' said Jimmy, being in that lady's employ.

'Say, what do you want for your monkey?'

'Nothing at all, thank you. He has more than is good for him already.' She turned back to Jimmy. 'Everyone spoils him in public, and I get the backwash of it in private, and have to discipline him.'

'Oh, Miss Thingamebob, I meant how much money will you take for him?' persisted Ydonea, raising her voice.

'One does not sell one's friends, Miss *What-you-may-call-'em*,' said Zarl, turning to the Elephant Hunter.

The perspicacious laughed to their interiors, but Ydonea was good-tempered as well as thick-skinned and ignorant – an undefeatable combination with beauty added. It accounted for her height on the golden ladder of industry.

'Do you put the little blighter out in the kennels?' said Jimmy, to ease the air.

'Indeed, no!' replied Lady Tattingwood. 'The dear wee fellow is an invited guest and has the room next to mine.' She, an heiress, married for her soap substance, was delighted with Zarl's repartee. Zarl could toss off the things that Clarice herself would have liked to say.

Cedd, commercially in attendance, tactfully observed 'I expect the acquisition of Percy will have to proceed like that of other stars. We could offer him a contract. Princes tout for them now.'

Percy having wrecked a thousand dollar confection with

the aplomb of the governing classes now complacently came to me.

'Do you go with the monkey? inquired Ydonea.

'Oh, yes. I have come with da leetle fellow. Alway. Da leetle monk he crya without me. I da coolie on da piece of string. I love mooch da leetle Percy.'

'Oh, Cedd, you must give her a contract too,' exclaimed Ydonea, clapping her hands. 'I'll say she's as 'cute as the monkey!'

'That's a wizard idea,' approved Jimmy, coming forward. He began to eye me. His expression indicated a straining memory. To elude its capture I excused myself on the score of Percy's needs and made an inconspicuous escape.

CHAPTER 7

Percy created equal excitement below stairs. He held court in a back corridor leading from the butler's offices to the servants' quarters. Even the butler took notice of him and was elated when Percy sparred playfully with him. Kitchen- and house-maids and others piled around as if he were a popular actor at the Chelsea Garden Party. In Ydonea's suite was an Indian with the form of him who 'trod the ling like a buck in spring,' whose legs were like water pipes painted white, and whose head was haughtily reared under a hefty turban of kalsomine green with a fan tail over the left ear. He had a coat of the same shade embroidered with golden leaves.

'Some rooster, ain't he?' whispered a house-maid. Nothing but the ballet skirts and war bonnet of a highlander with a beard on his knees, and a burr in his beard proper could have rivalled so spectacular a retainer. He regarded Percy with aloof disdain. He had the features and expression of some ruler on an ancient coin.

This was Ydonea's chauffeur. The friendly housemaid informed me that he had been presented to her by the young Rajah of Bogwallhoop. (This was her version of the nick- name given him by her master). He had been commanded to watch over Ydonea and the precious jewels till recalled from that post by the boss Rajah himself. 'And they say she can only keep the jewels while she remains pure. That's why she has to be so careful – her mother around her all the time, and kep' on ice so to speak. It ain't very modern, is it?'

'What you think – that a gooda plan?'

'All right while it pays, but a trifle dull. What do you think yourself?' She threw me a long knowing wink.

'You mean to be so pure, or so veree careful?'

My sociological tendencies were interrupted by the cook, who shooed us all to our pursuits, and I was left with the chauffeur, whose real name was Gulam, but Yusuf will serve to identify him. Ydonea called all her Indian chauffeurs by that name, as some mistresses call the office of footman Jeames regardless of its incumbent. I retreated from Yusuf's distinguished presence, trying to recall a resemblance. It came suddenly. This imperial creature had sniffed beside me in the Reading Room of the British Museum. English fogs had evidently distressed him, and he had sniff-sniff-snuffle-sniffed till I wanted to shriek 'Use your handkerchief!' His beauty had not reconciled me, for I had been reared to a complex that the proper use of handkerchiefs is indispensable good form.

Pooh! So the faithful and picturesque attendant presented by a potentate was probably a modest Indian student employing his week-end in earning a little extra money to pursue his studies! The Rajah and Maharajah were figments of Ydonea's publicity expert. Pooh!

Yusuf's beauty and sniffs had attracted me, but he had not deigned me a glance so I walked past him now saying 'Have you da handkerchief?'

He produced a shawl-like square of silk patterned as a tropic garden, smelling as the roses of yesterday.

'Da handkerchief for da use. This way, look!' I used a firm white one vigorously, and retreated with the parting shot 'Da Engleesh not lika da people not blow da nose, when da nose need da blow.'

I went victoriously to cultivate Mammy Lou, Ydonea's Negress maid. We began on a good level, she being exotic and personal maid to the great star, and I keeping up my end as foreign maid to a distinguished charmer with a popular monkey. Mammy Lou was a vast old darkey, genial and approachable as only Negresses can be. None of the flunkies could speak Italian, so the pidgin jargon I had assumed could not be questioned.

Mammy was probably an actress. She was a skilled

publicity agent. She welcomed me. I babbled artlessly about Percy. Mammy as artfully babbled about Ydonea. She showed her Mistress's jewel safe. It was not very large or heavy, but was locked with a chain to a big wardrobe trunk. The trunk in its turn was locked with a chain to the bedstead. A burglar could not therefore pick up the safe and walk out with it without shattering the trunk and bedstead. It was at present guarded by a stout man who sat on a chair with a revolver near at hand. I wondered if he might be a gangster. A second member of Ydonea's staff was posted under the window, and a gentleman, who had persistently ambulant movements for a guest, was frequently to be seen in the gallery approaching the door.

Mammy whispered that these were Pinkerton gennelmen who always guarded Miss Ydonea's jewels. I suggested that the real stones were probably in some bank, but Mammy raised her hands in pious protest. 'No, siree! I should say not, Miss Ydonea is the real genoowine article. If she says a thing, that thing sure is true.'

I persisted that it was unnecessary to carry jewels about to private house parties in England. Mammy mounted a big draught farm high-horse. It did not matter what the folks did in these out of date castles. Miss Ydonea had better ideas. She always wore her grand jewels on Saturday night. What was the use of spending all that money on jewels if they were not to be seen and used. Miss Ydonea believed in spreading the sunshine, not in gathering up cobwebs and dust on pretty things. I was dismissed as a dolt that had not read the papers. The Pinkerton man winked at me, and chucked Percy under the chin.

I attempted to lessen the worth of the jewels, but Mammy said that the blue diamond alone was worth five hundred thousand dollars. I adopted a more pacific manner and inquired if Miss Ydonea wore grand oriental brocade with the rajah's gems.

'Oh, naw, naw. That would be too ordinairy,' said Mammy, about whom I was now sure there was nothing Southern but her uniform and her name. She was a more practised actress than Ydonea, who had acquired her in Hollywood. 'Naw, my lawdy! Miss Ydonea will have a palest, pale sea-green silk embroidered in cream, and then she looks like a northern mermaid, and all the jewels, oh, boy! like the lights you see flash on the waves at Catalina Island.'

I was promised a glimpse of Ydonea when dressed. Other maids now appeared for a peep at the jewel safe, and Mammy Lou went through her piece again. Her only interest in Tattingwood, other than promoting her mistress's reputation, was a possible ghost. She was supplied with information that excited and terrified her. At a certain time of the year, according to contradictory authorities, or when there was going to be a death in the family, a ghost always paraded in the grand corridor. What shape the ghost took was not forthcoming.

Suddenly all the vassals disappeared as marvellously as young turkeys when Mommer Turkey announces a hawk, and I was face to face with the master of the house. The baron in his hall was as interested in Percy as the menials had been. Only the timid and the curmudgeon were ever above Percy's society.

'Oh, er, how did you carry the little blighter down?' inquired Lord Tattingwood, stopping to poke an affable finger under Percy's chin. Percy waved his arms like a wind-mill and made passes at imaginary monkeys in a way natural to him. His host grunted. 'Where will the little chap sleep? Must be careful he doesn't get out where one of the dogs will make short work of him . . . You are very fond of him, aren't you, my girl?'

'Veree, My Lord.'

'Pity we couldn't find you something better than a little devil of a monkey at Tattingwood Hall.' He looked at me with unmistakable amusement in his small cunning eyes.

'Percy sleep in da basket,' I volunteered.

'I should like to see,' remarked the gentleman, and it devolved upon a lady's maid to conduct him to our apartment.

He examined the waste paper basket lined with Percy's bedding. He was a man of simple interests, fond of shooting and hunting. He said there was a heavy footstool in his apartments which would make the scuttle quite safe as an anchor, and in a most democratic way took the hassock

33

already being used and proceeded to make the change himself. 'Come and see,' he commanded. We met the friendly house-maid on the way to Lord Tattingwood's rooms, which were at the other end of the grand corridor beyond the middle tower. The housemaid rushed to take the hassock. As opportunity occurred she winked at me and murmured 'The old chap's findin' his way home with you!'

'Da gentleman mooch interest in ma leetle monk.'

'Monkey, my eye!' she retorted, an uncompromising girl, and spry. 'You are not as used to these parties as I am. Sing out if you need any help.'

She deposited the heavy mahogany leather-cushioned foot-stool in Zarl's room and withdrew, again winking at large. Lord Tattingwood remained to place the foot-stool, and was apparently infatuated with Percy's antics. 'Tie the little blighter up,' he commanded. 'I want to see if he can move all that.'

Percy, when tethered, settled down in the glow of the fire with unusual placidity. Lord Tattingwood seated himself on a chair near by and without preliminaries pulled me to his knee. I remembered the housemaid's offer, but did not summon help. I eyed the poker near by and struggled to free myself. 'Oh, Mr. Engleesh Lord, ples, ples, I good girl. I pray da Virgin all da time. I tink I hear someone coming.'

That was efficacious. Lord Tattingwood resumed his game with Percy. 'Who's in there?' he asked, indicating the door into the Chief Inspector's room.

'The swell polissman,' I responded, critically surveying Swithwulf George Cedd St Erconwald Spillbeans, Sixteenth Baron Tattingwood. The eugenics of primogeniture had secured for him a coarse frame upon which sat a big red face with small eyes, a long ungainly nose, a narrow forehead and a sloppy mouth. He had one of those sandy skins, more often seen on dukes than barbers, and hair everywhere, even in his ears and nostrils. Ugh! On this had Clarice Lesserman sunk decent soap-suds money. What economics!

Thinking enviously of what I could do with a fortune of a few pounds, I murmured with genuine dejection 'I a poor girl!'

Swithwulf fossicked in his pockets and brought up half-a-crown. He proffered it, murmuring half to himself 'The old harridan keeps me deucedly short!'

Noblesse oblige!

'Half-a-crown no godda me.'

'Hum, you know more than you seem to, it strikes me. You're a dago, aren't you? Dagoes are hot stuff. One has to pay for what one wants these days – and the man who doesn't take what he wants, when he feels like it, and the cost be damned, is a poor man. Do you know enough English to get the gist of that?'

I shook my head. 'Da reech gentleman he must have what he wants,' I ventured.

He took a pin from his tie and handed it. 'Come to my room after dinner when they are looking at the shouties. You know where it is.'

He was gone out the door.

I popped out in his wake. 'Mista Lord,' I called, feigning breathlessness. He was already at some distance. 'Taka back – I honest. Perhaps I hava da monk and notta get away.'

'Tie the blasted little ape up,' he said, disappearing with astonishing celerity.

I returned to my quarters and examined the pin, a large pearl exactly like those priced ten bob at the Oriental Jewel shops.

Blasted little ape, indeed! More like a blasted big gorilla! And all that good soap-suds money wasted. What a life!

Quel gaspillage!

CHAPTER 8

I answered a knock on my door and found Captain Stopworth.

'There is a desire for Percy's reappearance in the lounge,' he said with a slight twinkle of amusement in his eyes, 'and as I was coming up, I have offered to act as his escort, and yours.'

We went down the grand romantic staircase together. The Chief Inspector was charming — now if he instead of Swithwulf . . .

He stood a moment looking down at the company lapt in that comfortable idle hour that stretches between tea and dressing for dinner, when men and women say the things that have to be said or listened to, in the hope of hearing or saying otherwise. The Elephant Hunter, by name of Brodribb, undertook to see to Percy so that he should not wreck the place. Deposited on the hearth rug, he was immediately another person. Studious, efficient, professional, he began upon his duties, the search for any unhygienic fleck or insect that might lurk within his reach. With his exquisite little hands he turned over the fur of a splendid bear rug which promised to occupy him indefinitely.

'You slip away and get your tea and amuse yourself downstairs,' whispered Zarl.

'Don't miss your tea,' Clarice added with a smile. 'Your little pet seems as if he could do without you for a while.'

Tea is a prosaic superfluity: at Tattingwood Hall as at a hostelry, a rare enchantment. I had the wonderful place almost to myself for an hour, till the dressing bell should summon those responsible for the physical cleanliness of the people disporting themselves so banally in the great hall. I peeped into the drawing-rooms, peered along galleries lined with armour, took the noble vistas with an enjoyment that was compensation for existence. One could almost feel the emotions that must saturate the beams and stones of such a pile, half-hear bygone laughter, rage or grief, like the echo of an echo escaping along the stately passages. What a theatre for lovers! How many had longed and lied there since the days of Elizabeth the Queen – from which in part it dated – to Clarice of soap, consoled for a dull lord by her handsome Chief Inspector. Well, great piles like Tattingwood Hall have been relinquished before to-day for romance, though such gambles are more glamorous when both parties to them are under thirty. Would the bulwark that Lady Tattingwood had secured against foolishness, hold?

I was too weary and cold to exert myself for my role in the comedy below stairs, so I slipped into Zarl's beautiful room where the big fire was so comforting. Zarl's things were spread towards the top of her bed, so without disturbing them I crept under the eiderdown at the foot, and aided by the warmth of the fire, set out to overtake some of the sleep which had of late eluded me. Just as I was gaining upon my desire, Lady Tattingwood entered from her room, accompanied by the Chief Inspector. Instead of passing into his own room, the Inspector turned the key in the door into the gallery and sat down with his friend before the fire. They sat in the glow of the coals which shone on the high wooden foot of the bed, but left me entirely in shadow under the eiderdown. They were comfortably settled before I had roused sufficiently to declare myself. I hesitated, and the only unembarrassing behaviour was to remain quiet hoping they would never know of my presence.

Clarice began to weep. She wept steadily and relievingly. Her companion let her alone for a few moments and then said 'Well, my dear, you don't seem very happy to see me.'

'Oh, but I am! The joy of having you here near me once more. Oh, Cecil, my darling!'

'We must be circumspect. This is very reckless of me now – if anyone came . . .'

'Oh, but they won't. They were all so entertained with that blessed little monkey. Did you ever see anything like it. And Zarl never rushes up to dress till the last moment. Her hair and skin and everything are so lovely and natural she doesn't have to spend hours in making-up.'

'Well then, I brought those letters as promised, but I want you to reverse your decision and let me keep them – they are precious to me, and some day in the future may be the most treasured possession . . .'

Their actions were reflected in the mirror on the dressing-table. Clarice leant toward him, and he put a kindly arm around her. 'You want our happiness to be known someday. You are not ashamed of it?'

'Oh, no. But your career has to be considered, and also Swithwulf's position.'

'All that he asks is to be let alone on his own trails. He is perfectly indifferent.'

'He might seem to be. But he is very cunning. He is not stupid. – . . . Oh, I'm so tired of Tattingwood and what it entails . . . I want to go away.'

'That is why it is foolish to run risks.'

'But I had to have *something* to carry me along . . . and this is a good opportunity . . . How is Denise?'

'More like her mother every day. She is always asking me about her mother. I have a struggle to evade her questions. Some day soon I must tell her the truth.'

'Better not. Young people are so conventional. She would feel disgraced, and never forgive.'

'A new generation has come since the war, and I am training Denise to have an open mind, so that she will be prepared. I discuss all sorts of things with her. I am teaching her to understand the romance of her parentage.'

'I am so weary waiting.'

'But I don't want to be marked as a fortune hunter. The money complicates matters.'

'Are you sure you really want me without the fortune? I am old now, and I often wake up in the night terrified, because I have been dreaming that you were only ridiculing me.'

'You must not make it difficult for me. You know there

has never been any woman for me but you. Surely my life has demonstrated that.'

'Oh, yes dear, and I am so grateful.'

'Well, trust me with these,' he tapped his pocket. 'My life must be uncertain, and I'll put these away in some vault in a sealed and locked packet, with a letter.'

'Oh, don't talk of that. It reminds me of the war. You can have the letters, but if Swith found them it would be fatal.'

'Thank you Clarice . . . Ssh!'

The Chief Inspector was gone to his room, with amusing speed. Lady Tattingwood attended to the key into the gallery, and then returned to her own room with slightly less dispatch. There were voices in the gallery, and I had just time to slide off the bed and switch on the light when Zarl turned the handle of the door. She was attended by the Elephant Hunter and Jimmy Wengham, who were in charge of Percy so that finger nails would not injure Zarl's trousered suit. Jimmy could not forbear to tease animals and children, Percy, catching sight of me, laid his ears back for a desperate effort which carried him with a whack to my shoulder, where his nails would have lacerated my skin but for the high-necked uniform. I snatched the lead, and the little creature snuggled to me with murmurs of relief.

'You, bad man. My little Percy he notta like you,' I said. After a little banter, the two men went away to dress. Percy had subsided and was lashed to the coal scuttle. He sat on the floor squawking softly and rubbing his nose with his hand. He was a trifle hungry, kept so expressly in order to be open to bribes.

Zarl was to wear my new dress, and no decorations whatever but Percy, just to contrast with Ydonea, who was to drip with trillions and crocodillions of jewels.

'I haven't a working wit, so I'm in the hands of my maid,' smiled Zarl, whose amenability makes her a delightful companion. The dress was a soft velvet, which glinted greenly in certain cross lights; a wrapped wisp to the knees, below which it flowed in undulations. It would disclose Zarl's perfectly fashioned arms and torso with bare-faced but well-grounded optimism, and heighten her 'ginger.'

'I hate my freckles,' she protested.

'There are none below the belt, so to speak,' I remarked, laying out her implements of toilet.

'You don't like Jimmy Wengham,' she commented. 'You would have liked him less had you seen him downstairs. He started cutting Percy's nails with that horrid dirk till they bled. I don't know what has come over Jimmy. He seems so brutal – I don't know how I could have carried on with him even for a minute.'

'Did you?'

'You don't suppose he'd lug Percy all the way from Africa in an aeroplane for me unless he had been infatuated. But he wants to go to excessive lengths in love.'

'How far?'

'Don't be such a peanut! He's sheerly sloppy. I've been telling him to reserve such mush in case he comes down in a desert atmosphere. England is mawkishly damp already. He always wants to go the whole engine!'

'Merely the usual, isn't it, nowadays?'

'It's carrying a cocktail like love altogether too far. Some men carry even a kiss too far, if they are not curbed. It shows a deplorable lack of imagination.'

'How far do you consider love can be carried without being too far?'

'Just to that point where the final demonstration to a person of imagination, would be a clog upon imagination.'

'I see . . . and the anticipation . . . you like that to inspire an expedition to the Antarctic or the Pole of Cold . . . I'm thankful Jimmy did not quite recognise me.'

'He wouldn't split if he did. Swithwulf has been telling me that he was right on the rocks. Clarice had to salvage him, and Cedd put him in the way of this job with the Zaltuffrie, to tide him over. He's mad to do a world flight, but he's such a cracked-brained thing that the aeroplane people won't trust him. He'd be likely to take off without his petrol or something like that.'

I confided to Zarl that I had found Clarice weeping when I came up. Seeking to discover if Zarl knew her secret, I asked 'Do you suppose it hurts her when old Swith tries to be gay?'

Zarl laughed right out. 'Really, you are too middle-class for a lady's maid among the best people. It comes of carrying respectability too far. Clarice is not such a goat with a cast-iron throat . . . If ever she did care, except from the point of hygiene and expense, she would have outgrown it long ago . . . Much more likely that Cecil has said something to her. I'd like to ravish that man myself, only I would never be mean to Clarice; but you've only got to look at them to see it could not hold up – why, she looks like his grandmother, and doesn't try to mitigate it.'

'If she had her face lifted, and dyed her hair, it would show weakness.'

'Clarice is weak. That is what makes her so lovable and kind.'

'Is this from Woolworth's, do you think?' I showed her the tiepin. She knows a little about jewels and antiques.

'It looks like a platinum setting, and if the pearl is as real as it looks it could be anything from fifty pounds to a thousand. Where did you get it?'

'Swithwulf George St. Erconwald Spillbeans Tattingwood gave it to me for *mes beaux yeux*. So while you have been adventuring, I too have not been idle. He has named a trysting place for this evening.'

'The *colossical* old reprobate! Clarice told me once that he humiliated her by his selection of ladies. She said if only he would choose someone like me she would not feel it such an unpleasant reflection, but I didn't think . . .'

'You didn't think it was so bad as a coolie on Percy's string.'

'I did not think he would have such discernment, or else your incognita is satisfactory,' bubbled Zarl. 'I'd just hang on to the pin if I were you. You are entitled to adventures among the best people. Their lives are an artistic struggle to escape from the drabness of carrying respectability too far.'

'You say that you picked it up, and return it to Clarice.'

'What are you going to do about the tryst?'

'What do you think?'

'That his optimism is barefaced, like the gallant Captain's who picked me for his lady for the voyage. Clarice will revel in this when the time comes to reveal it.'

'If ever it should.'

'We'll skip off home to-morrow. This mouldy collection of

oddments doesn't contain one man who could be pried loose from a life-size cigar or a bar parlour, except the Elephant Hunter or Jimmy, and each of those is more stony broke than the other, and each more luny. With people like that it takes altogether too much effort to keep them in the platonic form, whereas the nice professor scientists don't know what is the matter with them, but it works just the same . . .'

'Yes, like a donkey being lured on by a bundle of carrots on the end of the shaft, even unto the Arctic seas.'

'Exactly, but I did not construct the universe, and all things are there for our use. The difference between you and me is that I accept the world as it is, and you want to mess around and change it, and think it would or could be different if only this or that wasn't what it is.'

She was a delectable established fact in the green velvet. Her petite form had a lissom outline. Percy was attired in his black velvet evening shorts, specially designed for him by Madame Mabelle, with a white silk knitted singlet. We could not have buttons on the sides of the trews because he chewed them off, but there were glass buttons at the back to fasten the tabs over his lead.

Clarice entered to have a little chat with her friend before she descended to dinner. She wanted Percy to be present, and said that I could arrange for that with the butler. I agreed with alacrity. 'You are fortunate to have a maid so devoted to your little pet,' she remarked to Zarl, as I went out.

CHAPTER 9

There is room and to spare in the dining hall of Tattingwood to entertain an elephant or giraffe should the lord of that manor have taste for such guests.

We spread a sheet at one corner and brought in a small heavy garden table, and on it set Percy's tiny bowl of light ware, from which he would drink in his human ultra-dainty fashion. These jobs gave me an excuse to run up and down stairs while the guests were in their burrows dressing. As I turned into the great gallery from the tower stairs the Chief Inspector, already dressed, was ahead of me, evidently doing the rounds in his official capacity. His evening uniform was beyond sartorial censure, fresh yet easy, and his flesh glowed with fragrant health; a man to win any woman, and yet he seemed true to Clarice, the ineffectual, ten or twelve years his senior, and making no attempt to soften the disparity. There was dignity in the stability of this romance when compared with those that are as fleeting as barnyard *amours*. If he really did not desire Clarice's fortune, it was classical, even *colossical*.

I looked back after him and thus collided with a form coming in the opposite direction. It was the splendiferous Indian chauffeur, Yusuf. He was not a personal attendant and should have been with the other chauffeurs above the stables, long since converted into garages. He was, no doubt, prowling as guardian of the jewels, but I was so irritated by the impact that I boxed his ears and sped to Zarl.

It was time to descend. No trace of tears was now on Lady Tattingwood's hollow cheeks. An inner radiance transformed her, gave her gaiety and took ten years off her age. She was tastefully gowned in a quiet conventional style, and was a contrast for Zarl who looked like a mischievous elf in the extreme garment, with Percy wrapped in brown silk and held in the crook of her arm.

Mommer and most of the retinue were downstairs, but Ydonea was still awaited. She floated down the great staircase eventually to make an entry lifted unblushingly from the films, as sure of herself as a crowned princess in professional regalia. She approached slowly and regally and posed before one of the big fires in the lounge. Every male creature cavorted before her, casting covert glances or glaring, in key with his character. Cedd and Jimmy led the scrimmage, but business partly dictated their attitude. Even the Chief Inspector paid court, and his distinguished appearance exacted response from Ydonea. No woman could have resisted Cecil Stopworth had he exerted himself to woo. The more astonishing therefore was his faithfulness to Clarice. No wonder that people should doubt its reality.

Lord Tattingwood alone seemed impervious to the charms of the star. He winked at me, to whom Zarl had handed Percy, and as Percy was a dinner guest I had to be with him. Lord Tattingwood came ostensibly to pat Percy, but it was my arm he squeezed, and murmured something about the rendezvous. I considered what I could do to have the fun of storing my cake against another day.

Ydonea deserved her eminence. She was not entirely auriferous. She was more beautiful than is possible in reality. She dripped with ropes and plaques of gems, and on her head had a gaudy bonnet like a Russian royal head-dress that glittered like a looking-glass at every movement. Nevertheless she was more a spectacle than a siren. In the glances of the men was little of that which was in Jimmy's as he gazed on Zarl, the mischievous champagne-bubble lure of whose glances very nearly thrilled Miss Bitcalf-Spillbeans, who disliked Percy.

'Which jewels da rajah?' I asked Lord Tattingwood under cover of his interest in Percy. He evidently liked low company, and was quite matey with me.

'Whole box of tricks, except one or two, probably hired from a theatrical property man,' he grunted.

'Dey looka just as good.'

'One or two are real. That yellow diamond on a chain around her neck must be worth a ransom. Probably bought it from a dead-beat Russian. The blue one in the bracelet on her right wrist is genuine – could light my cigar by it. It is famous. There is a rumour that the Maharajah of Thinga-mebob is trying to recover it. The young cock gave it to the Zaltuffrie, and they say there are plots to rescue it – a yarn probably.'

He evidently knew something of jewels, had set himself up as one to be highly purchased by soapsuds, whereas I could only make soapsuds like an honest charwoman.

Everyone's mind was on the jewels and their fabulous worth. They brought a gleam even to the protective grey of the Elephant Hunter's orbs. 'Look at that blue one. If I had that I should be saved from bankruptcy,' he remarked.

'I'd be content with the yellow one, it must be worth two thousand,' said Jimmy.

'More like ten,' said Brodribb.

'Whew! If I had that I could raise the wind for my world flight, and she would never miss it. She could carry out the same effect with an imitation.'

'It's worth thinking about, Jimmy. Couldn't you get her to lend it to you?' said Zarl.

'It's certainly worth borrowing,' he replied.

Everyone passed into the dining room. Dinner was earlier than is usual at such places and put through with dispatch so that Cedd could show his original film. The jokes were poorer than the wine, the wit duller than the jewels.

Percy was delighted with his part of the meal, and immensely successful as a side show. He drank milk and water and had a crust of brown bread with a little jam on it.

When the diners rose I kept near to Miss Zaltuffrie.

The exhibition was to be closely guarded owing to her jewels, but nevertheless I determined to be present. The new film was probably of more interest to me than to most of the people present. I meant to gain admittance through Percy.

He was still of interest to Ydonea, and so dazzled by her display that he might have been a reincarnated pawn-broker. He danced at sight of the gems and boldly clutched them, seeing in them so many opportunities for trying his teeth.

Everyone passed towards the lounge with the exception of Miss Zaltuffrie, Jimmy and the Elephant Hunter. Wengham took the sheet that had been spread for Percy and jumped about with it.

'This would be wizard to play ghost, eh, what? Say Miss Zaltuffrie, they have a colossal family ghost here. Wouldn't it be coloss if he let you have a squint at him?'

'I'll say it would! – just colossical!' she laughed, annexing Zarl's word.

Jimmy cackled as he flapped his arms. 'I could nearly do a round-the-world flight in this.'

'I'm just crazy to see a sure-enough family ghost,' said Ydonea. 'Can't you raise one for me?'

'You wouldn't like the one here. He's a murderous old boy – appears only for something disagreeable, or out-and-out tragedy.' He turned to the butler and asked when the ghost had last been seen.

'Not for a generation, Sir. The night before the young master met his death by accident.'

Ydonea heard the story told me earlier by Zarl. I kept near to her as she went to the lounge.

'I don't want to see a mean ghost like that,' she commented. 'Jimmy is just the craziest thing! Always cutting-up so that I don't know when he's in earnest, or what stunt he'll throw next. But he's ever so 'cute!'

I passed her another chestnut for Percy, and this was even more enticing than the jewels. 'No often he lika one so soon. Verree, verree great luck – what you say, da mascot, when Percy he acta lika dat,' I murmured. When Percy clung to her (he clung to a chair leg when he objected to removal), she said he must sit beside her at the film show, and this was according to calculations.

As Jimmy Wengham came from the dining-room he detained me a moment by flinging the sheet over Percy, and while enjoying his frantic movements demanded, 'Say, I've seen you before with Zarl, haven't I? Has Zarl struck it rich that she can run to the personal maid business?'

'You must please ask Miss Osterley, please say nothing till she explains,' I began in a low voice, and ceased abruptly, finger on lips. Percy having extricated himself from the sheet, gave a warning guff, and the stately Yusuf was to be seen standing within earshot behind an armoured knight.

'Mum's the word all right. I'll see Zarl after the show. O.K.,' he said as we passed to the lounge because it was supposedly a warm room. Ydonea nevertheless felt the draughts which distinguish the best of English hospitality to the most ordinary American visitor, and Mommer said she must have a wrap. She went for it herself and invited me to accompany her to show the way.

'I'd trade a whole raft of this motheaten grandeur for a little American comfort and cleanliness,' she said when we reached the gallery. 'For the land's sake, I have to go along an icy hall a mile from my room to find a bath and lavatory. Can you beat it! I'll say you can't! What do you suppose makes the English like they are?'

'Probably da climate,' I ventured.

'Shucks! I should think the climate would kinda drive people with good sense in their heads to a few ordinary comforts. I didn't think a whole lot of their cooking. It needs a little something to digest it.'

To that end she secured a liberal supply of chewing gum of assertive aroma, as well as a fur wrap. When we regained the company she gave some of the digestive to Ydonea, who immediately proffered it to Zarl and the Elephant Hunter.

The fur wrap obscured a little of Ydonea's obscene glitter and made her increasingly attractive to Percy. He loves to nestle in fur, and better still to search it for particles of loose skin. No matter how full of 'lepps' he may be, he will immediately assume a professional air if there is a bit of fur, or a head, eyebrow or arm to be inspected. Never is he more fascinating than when his exquisitely fashioned little hands, with the perfect fingers and undersized inadequate thumbs, are instruments of research.

Ydonea was noisy with delight. I was firmly established beside her. She said Percy was a whole haystack of fun, and better than a muff to keep her hands warm. She let him chew her bracelets without qualms, while I sat in the next chair holding his lead and also a woollen scarf with which to extinguish him should be become obstreperous.

In addition to Ydonea's followers, already mentioned, were several prominent journalists and dramatic critics. These were augmented by after-dinner arrivals from the neighborhood, including a clergyman, a master of fox hounds, a retired general, a colonel, some scraggy women and some pretty girls. The new arrivals feasted their eyes on Ydonea's aurora borealis splendour. Her genuine beauty almost disarmed their snobbish prejudice, but the film magnates were a great satisfaction to prejudiced preconceptions. Mommer distributing chewing gum was such a fitting phenomenon that it oiled the superiority complexes to good humour. One old general regarded her gift with a haughty such-things-simply-aren't-done expression, but a M.F.H., bravely sporting, considered it would be cricket to accept Mommer's eupeptic efforts and gallantly went ahead till he became so entangled with his dental apparatus that he had to retreat from the room to regain normality. Miss Bitcalf-Spillbeans accompanied a blighting glance with 'Really! Reahlly, *reahlly!!!* The monkey must feel *quite* at home.'

This evidently inspired the Elephant Hunter and Zarl to private whisperings and to request extra sticks of chewing-gum from Mommer, which they chewed ostentatiously.

Zarl as well as Ydonea had a ring of admirers, though Zarl was thrown away on that company, and contemptuous of them. 'I don't know when I've seen such an unclassified collection of oddments,' she murmured to me. 'Like a jumble sale.' Zarl's forte is listening. She can listen so brilliantly to those worthy of her gifts, that after expounding themselves, great men have frequently been inspired to distinguished undertakings. Even commoner ones can be intoxicated by her attention.

'Say, Zarl, as soon as I see the little imps in your eyes, I could set out for the North Pole without waiting to collect my winter underclothes,' whispered Jimmy.

Cedd halted in his busiest moment to say 'It's inspiring to have you here Zarl.'

The siren and the spectacle. Carnal beauty and inspiring seductiveness were in contrast or constellation. Ydonea had no conversation beyond a few standardised pleasantries. The men followed her as a commercial bonanza in the hope of a surplus with which to purchase the seduction of a Zarl.

Cecil Stopworth was particular about seating the company because he and his staff were responsible for those jewels, and the room, which had a number of exits, was to be darkened. Two of Ydonea's private detectives, and Detective-Sergeant Beeton, and Detective-Constable Manning were re-examining windows and doors, and were finally stationed at the direction of their Chief. Cedd had retained two or three of his father's staff to supplement his own, and in addition, the only menials in the film hall were myself, Mammy Lou, and Yusuf, the Indian chauffeur. Stopworth insisted upon Yusuf being near one of the doors, where he himself was standing, and placed Mammy Lou in a front seat, where what light there was would fall on her. He permitted me to remain beside the star.

When he was satisfied with the doors and windows, he came to Ydonea and asked her in a low tone to entrust him with the big yellow diamond that hung at her throat. It was on such a slender chain that he said he would feel happier if he were its custodian for the next hour or two. He made his request with such a smile that I was more than ever enamoured of his charm. Zarl too watched his every move-ment. She was sitting immediately behind Ydonea, and beside the Elephant Hunter, who was on the aisle.

'He certainly is fascinating,' she murmured in my ear. 'I could almost go too far with him, but for poor old Clarice.'

'Is that fire really still alight?'

'How could it be? But one protects the illusions of one's friends. Cecil has got into the habit of philandering inexpen-sively and harmlessly with women above him financially, but he works too hard and has too little money to be dangerous. A mighty pleasant fellow at a pawn-broker's show like this. Clarice can let him do the worrying about the jewels.'

Ydonea removed her diamond without hesitation and handed it to the Chief Inspector, who placed it in an inner breast pocket. 'He's the 'cutest policeman I ever did see,' she remarked.

She was surrounded by protectors. On the other side of her sat Jimmy Wengham, by the aisle, immediately in front of the Elephant Hunter. Lord Tattingwood sat on the other side of me. He had so far not made any remark upon my defection from the appointment he had made.

When the Chief Inspector announced that he was ready, the film magnates hushed their loud technical conversation and seated themselves towards the rear of the theatre. The lights were then turned off. There was none remaining except that cast by the silver screen.

Clarice had been generous in helping her step-son with his career. His cinema hall was a drawing-room beyond the dining hall, fitted with seats on three tiers and with a fine screen and all modern devices. Something unusual was expected of Cedd. It was quite an occasion to be present at this showing. The film was prefaced by a formidable list of operators from the man who emptied the waste paper baskets to the one who guided the camera – not one was missed.

'The charwomen have been overlooked,' said Zarl. 'It is not chivalrous of Cedd.'

There was no suggestion of an author. Cedd was listed twice, as continuity expert and producer.

The film magnates clapped and guffawed. 'I'm sure going to enjoy myself,' one observed in a reverberating whisper.

'Clever Cedd,' murmured Zarl in my ear. 'He is selling himself as author under another name. What a tradesman he is, as well as an artist.'

The wonder of the blue diamond in Ydonea's bracelet could be gauged in the semi-darkness. It caught light from some source and glowed like a flame, now white, now blue. I missed some of the film shots to observe it. I missed still others through Lord Tattingwood's attempt to enjoy a petting party in the darkness, which was eventually retarded by a pin that caused him to start and emit a grunt.

'That blasted ape,' he muttered quite savagely, to cover his discomfiture.

Percy was restless, waving his arms and casting about after silhouettes so that I was thoroughly engaged. He was finally attracted by the gleam of the blue diamond, and Ydonea in her grand way unclasped the priceless band from her arm and put it around his neck.

'He can be the policeman,' she whispered.

Percy's fingers are so strong and deft that Zarl warned that he might pluck the stones from their setting. Ydonea said they could easily be reset. Percy was so engrossed with trying his teeth on the diamonds that I must confess to absorption in the film and carelessness with his lead. I was resting on the fact that he is very quiet in the dark.

Suddenly the leather rushed through my fingers following a warning guff from its wearer. Simultaneously with the disappearing leash, Ydonea arose shrieking that someone had hit her. 'They have taken my bracelet!' she called out. 'It has gone!'

'You were crazy to wear a thing like that here,' said Mommer.

'I'll say I was!' she agreed.

The lights did not come on as quickly as to be expected, seeing that Stopworth had stationed himself beside the main switch.

'Turn on the lights! Turn on the lights!' arose on every hand.

'Everyone remain quietly where he is,' commanded Stopworth.

Another voice explained that the lights had been turned off outside the room.

When the lights came on, the Chief Inspector's hair was disarranged and his face looked red, but he was thoroughly in command of the situation, and ordered everyone to stay put.

The only two who demanded to leave the room were myself and Yusuf.

'Everyone stay in his or her seat without moving, please,' again commanded the Chief Inspector, 'Till I can find out what has happened.'

'My bracelet with the blue diamond, someone hit me and grabbed it,' insisted Ydonea.

Zarl said that probably it was Percy that gave her a clout with his hind hands or lead as he leaped away with the bracelet. There was no accounting for the suddenness of Percy's 'lepps.' 'Find Percy and all will be well,' said Zarl aloud.

'Quite,' said the rasping voice of Miss Bitcalf-Spillbeans, the lady who had earlier asserted that monkeys could not be trusted. 'It's all some silly publicity stunt. Some people will do anything for a little notoriety.'

Yusuf was at the door begging excitedly to be let out to hunt the thief. He said he was guardian of the blue diamond, which was sacred, that the thief had escaped and he must pursue him immediately. Needless to say he was not allowed to go out, but was ordered to remain near Lord Tattingwood.

I wished to go out to pursue Percy, as a hurried search did not reveal him under any of the chairs nor behind curtains or pictures. Percy and the bracelet seemed to be missing. A roll call by Detective-Inspector Beeton and one of Ydonea's private guardians showed that no one who had been in the room when the lights went out was missing, except Percy.

'If he got out, someone must have got in,' observed Mommer Zaltuffrie.

'He could easily have gone out the fanlight,' said Zarl, pointing to it. This had been left open for ventilation. The great window on the front of the house was also lowered a few inches from the top.

Yusuf volubly upheld this. He knew the climbing capacity of monkeys. Percy could have run up the curtains beside the window like fire in a draught and disappeared in a moment. I had a vision of some dog worrying him. If not that, if he refused to come to our call, he would catch his death from chill. I was frantic to go out after him, but that was not permitted. Orders were issued for servants outside the sealed room to search for the monkey both in the house and grounds.

'Then let my maid be searched first,' pleaded Zarl. 'Percy will come to her, and when he is found all may be well.'

The Elephant Hunter and Jimmy were talking together apart. They approached the Chief Inspector with a request to be searched at once. 'If the monkey has the gee-gaw, it won't be safe for him to be at large, with us all cooped up in here, and we are the best two to liberate, as I know every bird's nest of Tattingwood, and Brodribb knows the jungle habits. He could mimic Percy so that Percy himself would be deceived.'

Protest against the suggestion of personal search arose. Such things couldn't be at a private house-party among the best people; such things simply weren't done – weren't cricket. Tattingwood Hall was not a seaside hotel for American tourists. If outsiders vulgarly displayed the contents of a jeweller's safe on their persons they should take the consequences and not subject delicately-reared ladies and gentlemen to outrage. But a number took the idea sportingly and demanded to be searched for their own satisfaction and a novel experience. Search it was to be.

Wengham and Brodribb were drafted off to a room adjoining to be examined by one of Stopworth's staff and one of Ydonea's. They were so long absent that it was remarked that search must approach dissection. Zarl pleaded for my early release. She was backed by Clarice, so I was the first female to be taken behind a screen to be examined by Mammy Lou, advised by one of the C.I.D. men. Mammy needed no advice. She was humiliatingly thorough. I doffed my clothes with an abandon warranted by my form and demanded that my person should be searched first. They could take as long as they liked over my garments. It did not flatter my character that Capt. Stopworth thought it necessary himself to examine my head, which he did with the skill of a barber and a dentist, and the manner of a gentleman.

I escaped in a sheet, which I had requested, and which Zarl had procured. It proved to be the one laid down for Percy during dinner.

Yusuf, owing to his insistence upon his knowledge of monkeys, was also speedily released to go after the wee absconder. He was waiting outside in the corridor when I emerged, hurriedly dressed in pyjamas and coat, stockings and shoes. Yusuf seemed less desirous of finding Percy than of chasing me everywhere that I chased Percy.

I skipped hither and yon, hoping to see him somewhere about. He was wearing a long lead, which would be a help. When he breaks loose without it we are helpless. Two or three hours of patience and industry have sometimes been

53

inadequate to recapture him in a moderate apartment and in a great place like Tattingwood it would be hopeless until he grew tired.

A demented race ensued. When I plunged into the long drawing-room and adjoining corridors, the chauffeur's shadow chased me like a jack o' lantern performance. If I dived into a room or cupboard, the chauffeur dived also. Again and again I protested against his rough methods. It seemed to me that the man was raving mad. Finding a broom with a heavy wooden head, I threatened to attack him if he would not search in some other direction. I raced up the stairs and along the grand gallery to our own apartment, thinking Percy might have gone there. Yusuf rushed with me. At my door I turned and menaced him with the broom. 'Go outside and look, please do. Don't act like a lunatic.'

'I know what I know. I must recover the jewel,' said Yusuf in cultured English, bounding downstairs after me. He evidently suspected me of wanting the gem as virulently as he did, whereas my only thought was for the misguided Percy Macacus Rhesus y Osterley. I turned on all the lights and called and coaxed and cooed through the big hall and dining room. I sat down and rattled nuts in my pocket, but no Percy came. I feared that he was loose in the cold. I scampered outside calling and good-fellowing, Yusuf still in my wake, excitement in his eyes.

CHAPTER 10

By ones and twos the people dribbled out of the sealed rooms, all eager to know if the monkey had been found. He had not. Nothing had been found by the search, but many tempers had been lost. Some unfortunate souls with physical secrets, who had suffered severe ignominy by such an overhauling, were asserting impolitely that the whole thing was a vulgar publicity racket egregiously engineered. Swithwulf the Baron took no pains to lower his voice. He said the onus of disproving the assertion was upon Ydonea, and that he would never have such rabble about the place again, not though they paid the taxes henceforth. He said to the Chief Inspector that it was all a hoax, but the officer was not to be deflected from strict professional routine.

It seemed as if Percy could not be in the house, and the Elephant Hunter and Jimmy Wengham – tardily released – led a search of the grounds. Zarl asked Capt. Stopworth to suppress Yusuf and everyone else and let her and me go softly about. If Percy were still in the house he might come to us. He was now probably thoroughly frightened and would not come out of hiding while strangers were about. He could very well be up in some of the dark beamed ceilings, or on an antler, or in one of a thousand hiding places. It was nearly as bad as trying to trace him in a forest. But if he were left in quietude his restlessness would soon induce him to reappear.

This was agreed upon. Zarl went in one direction, I in another. Presently there was a shout, 'There he goes!'

Someone had seen him shin down a bannister of the great

stairway and make along a corridor. Zarl was relieved to know that he was in the house. Everyone withdrew and I was allowed to follow alone in the direction Percy had taken.

At length, when I was thoroughly tired, I glimpsed the little silhouette sitting on the big sideboard in the dining hall. He had been seduced by grapes. He would sell his soul for grapes, and on the sideboard he found a hothouse bunch as large as cherries, enough to make any mouth water. His pouches were full to bursting, giving him the expression of an indecent old man with the mumps, and he had a berry in each hand. He was helpless with grapes. I shut one door and tried to get between him and another, moving gently because his lead was around a priceless epergne.

'Good fellow! Dear little Percy! Good little Percy!' I cooed. The sensitive creature was expecting reproval and showing his teeth in a pitiful grin. I was so glad to see him that I gathered him to me with tenderness, praising and caressing him. Relieved, he snuggled to me and began to ease the grape pressure with the aid of his thumb.

The Indian chauffeur swooped upon this reunion without ceremony, plucked the precious Percy from my grasp and began to undress him. Percy objected with spirit and dash. He screeched and clicked, struggling wildly to get free. He flailed the air like flying wire, and members of the company gathered to enjoy the fight between the chauffeur and me. Percy's trousers came away in the man's hand and something flew past and flipped on the carpet. Simultaneously the door from the Cinema theatre was flung open, the search of its contents having been completed. The curious crowded in there. I thought the flying object was a button, or one of the grapes, but the Indian flung Percy at me and went down on the carpet.

It was enlivening to the onlookers. The monkey came straight at my head, but was so excited that ere I could seize a limb, he sprang like a flying devil over several other heads – all too timid to act – and was gone.

Miss Bitcalf-Spillbeans, restated her dislike of monkeys, the foolishness of running risks of being injured for life by a 'horrid common little monkey.' They were degenerate creatures, she assured the company, and always treacherous. 'You never can trust them, *never*!'

'You don't have a monkey to trust,' said Zarl. 'A monkey is to fascinate. If you want an animal to trust, invest in a bull dog, or a turtle, or a cow, or a canary.'

Another lady, still harping in the earlier key, said that she had a brother scarred for life by a monkey. Lugubrious anecdotes accumulated.

Some spectators watched the groping Indian with interest while I took up the chase again. Exclamations announced Percy's route. He scuttled under most of the pieces of furniture in the big hall, his long lead partially retarding him as it coiled around things, but ere anyone could catch him he was running up the bannister. I pursued with unavailing blandishments. When the little debbil-debbil reached the first floor he turned and streaked down again like lightning. Zarl came to the bottom of the stairs while I remained above, both wheedling; and requesting strangers to remain at a distance. It seemed like an all-night job, but so long as Percy was not out in the cold the infatuated Zarl and I made no complaint.

He scampered up and down the stairs several times and then halted near the top. I stood in his way, and Zarl approached him diplomatically. He let her come within a few treads and then, as if fascinated by the old glass chandelier, turned and dropped with a tinkling clatter into its beads and festoons. Here he displayed the utmost composure. He threw back his head and averted his gaze haughtily as if bored to the back teeth by monkey worshippers, and was complacent because out of reach. Lord Tattingwood, whose evening arrangements had been impertinently evaded, ordered a step ladder while Zarl prayed that the tormentatious little black-guard would not wreck the heirloom from which he was suspended.

He did not like the look of the strangers gathering beneath him, and when Zarl extended her arms, showing him a chestnut, he sprang straight to her. She stood to the shock, despite her smart nudity, and this time we had him. His lead had followed him cleanly without disturbing a dangle of the chandelier.

There was no sign of the bracelet. People were theorising

volubly. Someone must have entered the room, or have been secreted in it, and really attacked Miss Zaltuffrie, as she asserted: that, they said, was why the monkey had been frightened and sprang away: his fright and flight had had a cause.

CHAPTER 11

Yusuf remained the centre of attention by creeping wildly all over the floor of the dining room, making the knees of his pipestem-like white pantaloons quite dusty. If he found what he sought, he kept it secret. He had the impudence to exclaim that I had picked up something as I was leaving the room. It was the button which Yusuf had wrenched off Percy's evening shorts. I produced it, on demand, from my apron pocket; and there was a button missing where I indicated. The chauffeur said I could have had the button from an earlier moment.

He crawled through into the Cinema Hall, like a big boy acting bear, and Zarl saw him pick an object off the back of the tall chair, the throne on which Ydonea had been sitting.

'Chewing-gum, I verily believe!' gasped Miss Bitcalf-Spillbeans. How disgusting, but it is in keeping. Throw it in the fire and have the chair washed.'

But Captain Stopworth commanded, 'Give it to me!' He took it in a piece of note paper, and carefully verified Yusuf's statement of where he found it. Brodribb, the Elephant Hunter, confessed that it was the gum which he had gallantly accepted from Mommer Zaltuffrie. The Chief Inspector asked Zarl where she had put her portion and she said she had thrown it in the fire.

Servants recommended by Lord and Lady Tattingwood were asked to assist the detectives in the search for the bracelet. If, as alleged, it had been carried away by Percy, it was plain that he had not been outside the house, and if not appropriated, the bracelet could be found by diligent search. The Indian chauffeur acted excitedly. He said that the rooms must be locked and searched one by one or the bracelet would be bagged by whoever found it.

Mommer, Ydonea, Cedd, the Elephant Hunter, Jimmy and others had this in hand. I was not much interested. Also I was otherwise engaged. Chief Inspector Stopworth was questioning everyone, and I was one of the first whose presence was requested in his room, next to Zarl's.

Zarl and I had managed a hurried consultation during the chase. In such a contretemps it was awkward that I was masquerading as a maid speaking broken English, but Zarl is not one to sell out on a friend. She does not squeal and throw all the cats out of the bag to save herself at the first hint of bother. It gives her marked distinction in a society largely composed of reneguers, no matter how assured their pretensions to 'good form.'

'Just let him question me as if I were genuinely a maid,' I said. 'The bracelet may be found presently and the whole thing end in a bottle of smoke. What is your theory?'

'Jimmy says it is only a publicity stunt, and he might know, being in the service. He says that chauffeur is engineering it. Or, if there is a genuine thief who startled the Zaltuffrie, Yusuf is making this fuss to cover the get-away.'

'What does the Chief Inspector think?'

'No one ever knows what he thinks when he is on a case. He is renowned as a secret worker. Never exposes his clues to be trampled by the herd. And he would have to take it seriously just in case it is not a publicity stunt.'

The Chief Inspector had arranged his room to give space, and look very much the office. The bed had been pushed in a corner and the writing desk brought forward and furnished with business-like materials. He was seated at it when I entered. His manner was unimpeachable and completely professional. Zarl had assured him that she could vouch for me, that I was her friend merely acting maid while I was depressed and down on my luck; which might have been a satisfactory explanation, or just the one to arouse suspicion. I had no way of knowing what the Chief Inspector thought of it, or me. He courteously bade me be seated, and greeted Percy, who was now nestling against me, glad to be comfortable and unreproved. He was eager to get to bed and so was I, as all the capering at high speed was fatiguing.

The Chief Inspector asked my name, and when I replied Ercildoun Carrington in plain English, made no comment. He asked my business or profession, where I lived and all that sort of thing for a beginning, and then said. 'I should like you as clearly as you remember to show me where the monkey was when Miss Zaltuffrie cried out that someone had hit her, and tell me what were your movements and the movements of other people until the lights went on. Did you return to your own room during the hunt for the monkey?'

'Several times.'

'I shall have to order the room to be searched. I shall close the doors and windows now.'

'Please do.'

I stepped with him into the room and he turned on the lights. His quick trained glances travelled around taking in details, and he stooped and picked up the pearl tiepin given me earlier by Lord Tattingwood. Percy must have flipped it from the mantlepiece as I brought him in.

'Is it valuable?' I asked, as he examined it.

'Don't you know?'

'I know nothing about gems.'

'How did you come by it?'

'I saw Lord Tattingwood wearing it. He must have dropped it when he was in here looking at Percy before dinner.'

'Perhaps the monkey pulled it from his tie,' he remarked, as he pressed a bell.

'In this case *not* a publicity stunt.'

'Neither may it be in the other.'

'Quite! And if Percy really sprang away with the bracelet, it may still be lying about, and I should like to be free to look for it myself.'

'And if it is not found, what then?'

I did not let prejudice against Yusuf, because of his sniffing in the British Museum, bias me into mentioning his name, but I said 'Watch that person who tries to put blame on others.'

'And that is . . .'

61

'That will be noted as the case ripens – if it isn't merely a bottle of smoke.'

'Have you had any training in criminal investigation?' he inquired, looking keenly at me.

'None, but I should think that common sense and observation would greatly help the untrained.'

'Ask Lord Tattingwood if he will be so good as to come here for a moment?' said the Chief Inspector to the servant who answered his summons. He made sure of the fastenings of the doors and windows, and returned to his office, leaving the door from Zarl's room open.

'I want you to tell me exactly what happened when Miss Zaltuffrie raised the cry.'

'I sprang up to grab Percy. He had been on Miss Zaltuffrie's knee. I was beside her holding the leash, which he dragged out of my hand. Lord Tattingwood was on the other side of me. He growled. "Keep steady! Don't run amok like a herd of elephants!" A few people seemed to be moving about, but around me there was not much commotion till the lights went on.'

'And now tell me exactly how each person was sitting or standing or acting generally, near to you, when the lights went on. Be as exact as you can.'

'Lord Tattingwood, Miss Osterley and I were seated as we had been when the lights were turned off. Miss Zaltuffrie had risen, but she sat down again and her chair was slewed around a little. Mr. Wengham was pushing his way amid the chairs to her.'

'Are you sure of that?'

'That is what his action looked like. He leaned over her tall chair caressingly as if to protect her, but the Elephant Hunter was before him.'

'And where was Mr. Wengham sitting when the lights were about to be put out?'

'Beside Miss Zaltuffrie, on the aisle, and the Elephant Hunter behind him again.'

'You are observant and have a clear memory,' he remarked, 'but are you sure that Brodribb got to Miss Zaltuffrie before Mr. Wengham, who was seated nearer?'

'Yes.'

Swithwulf, Sixteenth Baron, here presented his long heavy nose and small embedded eyes.

'I shall want you to come downstairs later and go over this again where it happened,' said the Chief Inspector.

'Anything I can do for you?' inquired Lord Tattingwood, regarding me with inimical suspicion.

'Merely that you might help us with a clue. How were people sitting when the lights went out . . . and by the way, is this your tiepin?'

'I'd have to look at it first. Where did it come from?'

'I found it on the floor next door. You probably dropped it when you were visiting the monkey before dinner.'

'Me! I, here, looking at the monkey! Who says I was here?'

'It seemed an explanation of the pin's presence.'

'Who said it was found here?'

'I found it myself.'

'That is no reason to jump to the conclusion that I was here too.'

'His Lordship's memory is not good,' I interposed.

'Do you categorically deny being here before dinner?' asked the Chief Inspector.

'Certainly. I went straight to my room to dress, I remember because I was late.'

The Chief Inspector wrote a chit swiftly and gave it to the man outside his door. Then he turned to Lord Tattingwood and held out his hand for the pin. 'Thank you, Lord Tattingwood, and you do not recognise this pin as yours?'

'I have one that is like it, but I could not be sure if this is it unless I saw whether I had another or not.'

'I should be much obliged if you will ascertain.'

'Certainly. I'll go at once.'

Was the old fool afraid that I should divulge what had brought him to call upon Percy, or was he just one of those sneaks that acts thus under pressure? Supposing my life or liberty depended upon his speaking the truth! Such behaviour from a man of his family and education was discouraging to any but a political irreconcilable.

The Chief Inspector made a note and put a few more questions till Lord Tattingwood returned. 'I cannot find my pin anywhere, so that must be it,' he admitted.

'How do you account for it being here on the carpet?'

'That and the disappearance of the bracelet will be interesting for the police to solve. One does not know what riffraff comes to the house since the war.'

'When did you last wear the pin?'

'I don't remember. I'm rather forgetful. Probably I left it sticking in one of my ties.'

'If you should remember, you will be good enough to inform me.'

'Oh, er, certainly. I'll give you every assistance in my power. You'll find whoever took the pin has the bracelet also.'

Lord Tattingwood retired. The Chief Inspector asked 'What have you to say about the divergence between Lord Tattingwood's evidence and your own?'

'He's a gentlemanly old soul! What chance has the word of a coolie on the end of Percy's string against that of a Baron?'

'It depends on further evidence to prove which is lying,' said he, quite impersonally.

Zarl was the next to be questioned, and she came with Clarice. I told Zarl in a whisper, while Lady Tattingwood was saying something privately to the Inspector, how Lord Tattingwood had denied visiting Percy. 'Mean old toad, I never gave a hint of his improper advances. He could surely have admitted coming to look at Percy. Everybody always comes to see him quite innocently.'

'Ah, but Swithwulf never goes to see any woman in your present walk of life innocently. He knows they would all see through the Percy camouflage, and that is why the poor old cow was so scared that he lied. I must tell Clarice; she will understand.' Zarl turned to her, picking up the pin from the Inspector's table. 'Look,' she said 'Captain Stopworth found this pin on the floor of my room and Ercil says that Swithwulf must have dropped it when he was here just before dinner talking to Percy, but Swithwulf says that was impossible because . . .'

'I dropped it myself,' said Clarice promptly. 'I had it stuck in my dressing-gown. I'm so glad it is found.'

I flirted my eyelids at the Inspector, but he was grave as a sculptured image of the old gods. It was most sporting but a little excessive of Lady Tattingwood until she should have heard the whole story.

'Lady Tattingwood never lacks courage, and her generosity is well known,' remarked the Chief Inspector, giving her a glance which I liked. He dismissed me for the present, saying that I could search for the bracelet, but that he would require me later in the cinema hall.

CHAPTER 12

Cedd Spillbeans merited condolences that the showing of his film had gone so ill, perhaps had lost the chance for which he had worked and manoeuvred, but he was a gentleman in the matter. He was aiding the detectives and attending to the requirements of guests wherever possible. Those from the neighborhood were loath to go home till they heard the end of the exciting comedy, and those in the house were too excited to retire for hours yet.

Ydonea was acting prosaically. She quickly felt the breath of unpopularity blowing her way, and did her best to counteract it. 'I'd like to get the bracelet back if possible, but I don't want anyone to be worried about it. There are just as good pebbles at the jewellers as ever came from them, to date.' She was only twenty-three and had not yet known reverses.

Hostile members of the company said that her carefree attitude was vulgar ostentation similar to that of lighting a cigarette with a ten-pound note. Others said it clearly indicated that the whole thing was a publicity stunt and that the bracelet had been passed to someone of her retinue during the hubbub. Had the detectives been searched?

I was suddenly sick of these people, as well-groomed as prize beasts at a fair, but most of them petty or mediocre or worse under test. I was shut out of my room till it was searched and I could not now go to the Servants' Hall. I stole about the place with Percy in my arms seeking a nook wherein to anchor for a little rest. The search for the bracelet was still proceeding, and also the examination of various people by the Chief Inspector or his colleagues. Ydonea's private men too were quite officious. Eventually I found a little den beyond the drawing-rooms. It had a gas fire, to which I put a match and then sank into a big, easy chair. Percy is always cuddly and manageable in the dark. Old Mother Monk had evidently instilled into him the need to be careful after dark.

In two minutes he was fast asleep. The greedy little wretch had been unable to swallow all his grapes, and one or two were still extending his pouch. His endearing abandon, spread on my chest, his tiny clinging hands, the fragrance of his person, his furry warmth comforted my harried soul. He was nervous and started and shuddered in his sleep as I placed a scarf about him with tender touch. I laughed at the suspicions he had directed towards me.

Too disturbed to doze, after a few minutes relaxation my mind began upon the disappearance of the bracelet. I recalled that before the leash had slipped through my fingers, Percy had made the little warning guff that he always gives when a stranger, and particularly a male stranger comes near him. Someone inside the room may have sneaked up to seize the bracelet under cover of the darkness. He may have got away with it. Otherwise, Percy must have carried it with him as he escaped through the fanlight. He had a habit of hanging on to quite large objects tenaciously for a considerable distance when chased. He could easily have carried this one to some high nook where it might lie undisturbed through extended search. He could climb like a rat or beetle, and the great apartments bristled with embrasures, curtain rods, ledges and crevices. Or, if the publicity theory were correct, how long would Ydonea keep it up. She would hardly like to confess now; and unpleasant suspicions gathered around several people, including me.

Speculation hovered around the chauffeur. If taking part in a publicity stunt, and merely acting, he could simulate the hungriest glare I had seen in human eyes for a long time. He seemed genuinely feverish lest someone would be ahead of him in recovering the gem, and with undisguised frankness he suspected that person to be me. It was within the bounds of possibility that he had been set to guard the gem by someone. That someone might be the Rajah of Wobwollah, or whatever it was, though when one knows to what even the top-most film stars have to resort — mustering sheriffs to get a dinner with a Lord Mayor, and paying visits to Dukes and dungeons — it is difficult to believe or disbelieve.

Then there suddenly flashed into my mind the cause of a certain noise which had reached me as I emerged from being searched. I looked down at the tiny sleeping face so confidently snuggled against me. When the cruel, self-indulgent character of human association with animals is considered, it is profoundly touching that any beast or bird can be so generous and brave as to treat one as an equal and a friend.

'My little peanut, I am sorry to disturb you, but I've just thought where you may have left the bracelet, and if it is there, all this fuss and bother has been your joke on your inferiors.' Percy guh-guh-guhed and shuddered in irascible protest, but I carried him upstairs and requested a few words with the Chief Inspector.

'There are three possibilities about the disappearance of the bracelet,' I postulated. 'One is that it was carried by Percy to some place, and if that proves true, the other two can be wiped off the slate. I heard a little noise when I first came out of the cinema hall, and the bracelet may have made it; will you come with me and look.'

He consented, and left his office in charge of a subordinate. I explained that Percy, before he was captured finally, had sprung on to the chandelier with such assurance that he might have been there earlier, and deposited the bracelet. The noise I had heard could have been the tinkle of the glass stalactites.

We were careful not to attract attention as we stood looking down on the chandelier. There amid the festoons of glass prisms hung the bracelet. It was so conspicious that it was inconceivable that it could have passed unseen for the hours that had raged since its disappearance, but a monkey is unsurpassed to distract the eye from other activities and objects. Everyone had been interested in the capers of Percy to the exclusion of other things. Either that, or it *was* a publicity stunt, and some member of Ydonea's retinue had tossed the bracelet there after the removal of Percy.

The Chief Inspector took the honour of the find. He mounted a long step-ladder to retrieve the bracelet. As he took it in his hand Yusuf sprang from somewhere yelping 'The blue diamond in the centre has gone!'

If he was acting, he was a master. The excitement in his eyes was fanatical. My heart missed a beat at the implication of his words. The diamond gone, and I the one to lead the Inspector to the lost bracelet! I wished that I had not been so smart at deduction as to the whereabouts of the lewdly useless and troublesome bauble.

People quickly gathered. The recoil upon me was swift. Yusuf looked up and saw me leaning over the bannister. He lept towards me exclaiming, 'I knew from the first that she took it. The monkey swallowed it. That is what he was brought here for. It is a common trick in India, and this woman has trained him. I see it at first glance. Here you have a wily adventuress. That air flying man is her confederate. I heard them in conference just after dinner.'

I did not linger to combat this. I fled to the Chief Inspector's room, and Detective-Sergeant Beeton for refuge. Zarl was there awaiting further questions.

'The putrid old bracelet has been found but without the middle piece of glass, and that foul chauffeur thinks Percy or I have swallowed it – you don't think it too, do you?' I elucidated.

'Why, where, what, how? It doesn't matter what you have done. I can get the rights of it some other time,' said Zarl springing to me, a full-fledged and unquestioning ally, and dragging me through the door into our room, where a search was proceeding. That was the kind of companion to warm the heart in a world of Swithwulfs and Yusufs.

Yusuf thumped on our door and shrieked that we must not be allowed to escape, that we were both wily adventuresses. He was sharply ordered by the Detective-Sergeant to put himself under control lest he should be placed under restraint.

The Chief Inspector tapped on the door authoritatively. 'Come out Miss Osterley and bring your companion.'

Zarl replied that she was willing to come out, but not to risk an assault upon Percy from anyone, for any putrid mouldy old jewellery, whether it was a Kohinoor or a Woolworth string of beads. She also gave her opinion that it was much better taste to wear Woolworth's pretty things than some trash that was dangerous to the lives and comfort of innocent and respectable people. She demanded the full protection of the law for herself and her maidservant and her pet, and also stipulated that we were all three to be treated as innocent until we were proven otherwise.

The Chief Inspector reminded her that that was his unfailing procedure and that nothing was gained by resisting the officers of the law, but Zarl muttered that it was safer to be an intractable vixen than a charmed rabbit in any circumstances. With her psychological monkey up to her eyebrows in rosy flushes, and her African monkey in the crook of her arm, his funny little face full of boredom with the whole performance, she was such an engaging fury that I chuckled like an Australian kookaburra regardless of propriety. This was fortunately put down to hysteria. There was interest and amusement in the Chief Inspector's eyes as he regarded her. His voice was silky as he informed her that it was necessary to proceed in accordance with the fresh development in the disappearance of the diamond.

Zarl handed Percy to me, as, being relieved of his fears, he had set about the major morality of his existence and was assiduously investigating some little moles or marks on her half-nude form.

'There is certainly something degenerate in monkeys,' remarked a familiar voice. It was Miss Bitcalf-Spillbeans. 'I should hate a monkey to be so fond of me. It wouldn't look well.'

'I don't think you need have any fears on that score,' said Zarl sweetly.

'Dreadful little monster, what a bother he has created! They say they never live through an English winter, and I should think you would be relieved when he dies.'

'All my acquaintances and a number of so-called friends would relieve me more by dying,' said Zarl.

The Chief Inspector was now before his desk, everyone but Zarl, Yusuf and me excluded. Yusuf repeated his accusations. The blue diamond was of legendary reputation and cost — sacred. He suspected that the monkey had been brought there to help in stealing it from the first, and now his suspicions had proved correct. Percy might have come from Africa, but he immediately recognised him as Indian. Stopworth told Yusuf that what he said had been noted and gave him over to Detective-Constable Manning for the present.

Zarl said she would mobilise the Elephant Hunter and Jimmy as a guard for Percy, adding that men should be a little useful as well as unornamental. The delightful Chief Inspector and I were left together. It was almost worth the hullabaloo to have such fascinating association.

'Take a seat,' he said courteously. He then ran over some of his notes. 'I understand that you have been doing publicity work for a certain prima donna, and before that you investigated travelling conditions for migrants going to the Overseas Dominions.'

'Quite!'

'And that you came here as maid to Miss Osterley to help her with her monkey, and to keep up her end against Miss Zaltuffrie.'

'Exactly. And this mess spoilt our little plot, gave me the limelight, which I do not need, and took it from Ydonea. If I could have done this for some of my clients, my fortune would be better than it is.'

'Am I right in thinking you are in very low funds?'

'You would always be right in thinking that, but it is not a danger to society, because I am not avaricious.'

'I wish you to know that I have proved that you were speaking the truth about the tiepin being here, not the whole truth, but some of it.'

'Do you mind telling me how you proved it?'

'I saw Lord Tattingwood emerging from your room before dinner. One of my men ascertained from his valet that Lord Tattingwood was wearing that pin this afternoon: besides, I recollected the pin at tea time. It was a little large and pink for . . .'

'A Sixteenth Baron – more like a film magnate?'

'Exactly! So you see.'

'I see: rather bad though if my life or reputation had depended on the Sixteenth Baron's evidence.'

'We all run such risks, and worse, in human association. I see little else.'

'I suppose you believe in nothing else.'

'The little else, by comparison becomes the most precious thing in human association.'

'Like Lady Tattingwood's readiness to go bail about the tiepin.'

He would not let me share that. 'Lady Tattingwood has probably been using the pin recently, as she stated ... It was sporting of you not to hint why the gentleman visited Percy ...'

'Pooh! *That!*'

'What are your suspicions?' he asked me suddenly.

'Suspicions can be very cruel,' I parried. It would be mean to confess that I suspected Yusuf because he had irritated me to loathing by his sniffing in the British Museum Reading Room. That he was a student as well as a chauffeur *pro tem* was not illegal. It was commendable. The police had every facility for tracing him, so I decided to let that pass.

'I never act on suspicions ... they are sometimes useful in furnishing a clue ... what do you think of Yusuf's accusation that the monkey has swallowed the gem?'

'I have never known him actually swallow such an object. He often seizes a button, and once took a thimble and another time a big peach stone, and got into difficulties. He is extraordinarily clever at retaining a smaller object – can put it from his mouth to his pouches again and again without swallowing it, or spitting it out. As soon as I saw the blue diamond was missing from the setting, I thought that might have happened, and also that he might have swallowed it in the hurry of the chase. I meant to be careful in recovering the thing. Percy could not harm it and I should have given it to you to return to Miss Zaltuffrie.'

It had seemed as simple as that to Zarl and me at the time, but we were ignorant of finance, and how many persons go off their axis criminally where gems of the notoriety of Ydonea's are concerned.

'Your own life would be in danger during such a process, and Percy would soon be no more,' said the Chief Inspector.

'I fancied that Percy ground something between his teeth after I caught him, but a piece of coal which he brought to light might explain that, but I know the genius of his fingers too well ever to allow him even sixpenny jewellery. Could I not be incarcerated under observation with Percy where I should be safe? It would be ignominious, but I'd do anything to save Percy from harm. All this mess has happened through bringing him to spend a week-end with the best people to save me from the woofits, and it devolves upon me to see him through.'

'It is at least a sporting offer,' said Stopworth with a smile, 'though it has a fishy side.'

'You mean that I could have handed the gem to Zarl long since?'

'That, or half a dozen other possibilities.'

'In such case I demand that Yusuf be shut up too till the gem is recovered from his own body or from Percy. Also, if the Zaltuffrie crowd are not "throwing" a publicity stunt, and if the gem is not found in Percy or Yusuf, someone else may have escaped with it.'

'That possibility is being acted upon,' he said, a little coldly. 'My men are very capable.'

'Miss Zaltuffrie says they are the 'cutest policemen she has ever seen,' I said as a parting thrust, confident in virtue and honesty.

CHAPTER 13

Ydonea, Yusuf and others took their turn in the moving picture under Stopworth's direction. Some of us were assembled to reconstruct events in the cinema hall. Yusuf immediately placed himself near Percy, who was in Zarl's arms, she being protected from his clambrous embrace by a velvet coatee.

'Quit your monkey shines, Yusuf,' admonished Ydonea. 'Leave them to Percy. I guess there are scads of ways of tracing the doggoned old diamond, and with a whole lot more kick to them, than throwing duck fits in an ancestral castle.'

She cast a duck's eye or two at the Baron himself, but rather as a matter of form. Such reflexes had been standardised for her by a man with a megaphone. And all members of family and houseparty tacitly understood that no one should obtrude upon Cedd's patter till a film was put through. Cedd was fighting for his career, which in England has a recognition as sacred as the cow in India. Also Ydonea's Mommer-Mrs.-Grundy complex was reported to be 'genoowine.'

The Elephant Hunter and Jimmy Wengham made play as Percy's bodyguards, for the pleasure of being near Zarl. 'Nothing but the majesty of British law itself shall lay a hand on him,' said Jimmy. The Elephant Hunter said nothing. He kept his cold grey eye on Zarl as if she were an African animal or a target.

Yusuf and I were the main antagonists. He had such a fanatical desire for the return of the blue diamond that he

74

seemed to think nothing should be allowed to stand in his way.

The Chief Inspector announced that I admitted the possibility of Percy having swallowed the gem, in which case there would be no need to waste the time of his Department further in the matter.

Ydonea gained in my regard by saying unaffectedly that she did not want the 'cute little monkey to be hurt, that she would rather lose the crazy old diamond outright than endanger him. 'I *must* have him for a picture now! Cedd, put him in one. Make him a continuity. Can't you see that he attracts more attention than all the rest of us put together. The picture to-night seemed to be developing kinda dull, not enough pep.'

'This would be more in your *genre*,' said Stopworth with a disarming smile.

Zarl was growing reconciled to Ydonea as a quite human female whose asphyxiating beauty was harmless because an extra-territorial phenomenon.

'Couldn't the silly business be settled by X-Rays to save waiting – and danger to Percy?' enquired Zarl. Her jaws were set on that. We wouldn't have had that mischievous little monkey, weighing six pounds, injured or tormented for a diadem, and any man of understanding respects such a situation, or else so many of those offensively moron goggle-eyed Pekes and Poms wouldn't remain alive in a dense population of nervous people.

Lady Tattingwood suggested the excellent X-Ray apparatus at the Supersnoring Home for Cripples. She had helped to run a hospital at Tattingwood during the war, and had been Hon. Treas. of this Supersnoring Hospital ever since. It was only a mile from Tattingwood gates. Stopworth agreed to this proposal, and Clarice went away to telephone.

Jimmy Wengham offered to take Zarl in his Austin Seven (geared for Brooklands) in which he had rattled down from London, as England's protective invisibility had been against air passage.

'What ho! If only I had my air 'bus it would be useful now,' he remarked.

'What for – to escape with the loot?' inquired Zarl, while the Elephant Hunter never took his eyes off her.

Lady Tattingwood returned to say that the operator at the hospital would take the photographs as soon as the patients arrived. Yusuf and I were ordered to prepare ourselves and go in the local police car. There was no love lost between Yusuf and me. He was so eager to track the diamond to me that I felt sure he must have something to do with its disappearance himself.

Zarl said she would go too. 'I shall not trust Percy to any stranger while Miss Carrington is being photographed.'

'You are just like an old woman with a poodle, with that stinkin' little cow,' said Jimmy, who had assimilated the Australian significance of this noun as an epithet.

'He smells much nicer than you,' retorted Zarl burying her face in Percy's back. Thus disturbed he flung his arms around her neck and gave her a delectable kiss.

'Well, I'm dithered! Can't you get something better than that to kiss at Tattingwood?' remarked Swithwulf.

'Do you suppose women would take to poodles if there was anything better?' said Zarl, handing me Percy. 'You must take the old lady with her monkey,' she twinkled at Stopworth. 'If the diamond is found on me, I want to be arrested by you. Clarice, you come too to chaperone me while I am put through the third degree.'

We went upstairs for our coats. 'Nice little treat for poor old Clarice,' said Zarl. 'Anything would be an improvement on being stalled with these oddments.'

The local police, apprised of happenings, were alert to the movements of anyone around Tattingwood Hall or the neighborhood. We set out in a local car with a local driver, with a C.I.D. man beside him. The Chief and I had the corner seats at the back with Lady Tattingwood between us, and Yusuf and Zarl facing us on the flap seats. Percy was in my bosom. Zarl was sleepy but struggled to be alert lest Yusuf should fall upon us with some magic of the East and eviscerate Percy instanter.

Stopworth returned to the hall to say something to one of his staff and Jimmy leaned through the window to murmur to Zarl. He was in full flying kit and was disappointed that Stopworth refused his offer to escort us.

'Seems to be liftin' a bit. I might blow up to London and bring the Moth down and do a few stunts to-morrow, or I might start on my flight to South America,' he remarked aloud.

Zarl advised him to wait for better weather, but Jimmy said when it was summer above the Line it was winter below, and he preferred to have the balmy hours at the other end of so long a stretch.

'Whatever I do it will be for your sake, you must always remember that,' he finally whispered, with melodramatic inflection.

'I don't accept any such responsibility,' Zarl whispered in rebuttal.

The X-Rays exonerated Percy, Yusuf and myself. The plates when developed might divulge more, but the doctor said there was no famous diamond to be discerned, certainly not in the organs of Percy.

Yusuf was unappeased. His suspicions took a fresh turn. He said there was a plot in which the Chief Inspector was concerned. How did anyone know that the Chief was from the C.I.D. at Scotland Yard? Yusuf apparently had found English institutions unworthy of trust, or his mind may have been inflamed by film romances about jewel robbers and their aristocratic connections. He lost his head and said many abusive and silly things. Zarl asked Stopworth if he couldn't arrest him. Stopworth said not unless someone liked to lay a charge against him.

The household was still up. Even the neighborhood guests had not departed. Cedd had had a trying time. He had offered to proceed with the interrupted film display, but Ydonea said she could not concentrate. The otiose film magnates seemed utterly disconcerted by encountering a familiar film story in real life, and the cool questions that were put to them by Scotland Yard officers. The icy politeness alarmed them. They did not know what to make of the affair and congregated in the smoking-room and performed on their exceptional cigars. It was well that Cedd had such a weakness for Zarl, as he had just grounds for irritation in her pestiferous little ape which for the moment had frustrated his plans.

People had been too nervous to sit again in a darkened room, so they had made loud unspontaneous whoopee in other ways. The butler was waiting his mistress's return to serve a sumptuous supper, including lobster salad.

The Chief Inspector took me and Zarl to his office, and, because Yusuf had been so rude to me and so venomously suspicious, I mentioned now that he had occupied a seat beside me in the Reading Room of the British Museum and that I had particularly noticed him because of his sniffing. Yusuf was called in, and Ydonea summoned, and when the former had retreated, the latter confessed that he might not be her usual chauffeur. 'But it is hard to tell those men apart. Coloured folks all look as much alike as peas in a pod,' she said.

Yusuf had a ready explanation. The usual chauffeur had been taken ill with cramps, and Yusuf, being very like him in height and appearance, had stepped in to save a good job for a fellow countryman.

Thus his excitement about the jewel could only have been simulated. His passport was in order, his surname was Das, or something as commonplace in India as Martin in France or Robinson in England. The Chief Inspector did not attach so much importance or irritation to Yusuf's sniffing in the Reading Room as I did. It was impossible to guess what the Chief Inspector thought important, or if he had discovered any useful clues.

He detained me when the others withdrew. 'The X-Ray business has not helped towards a solution of the disappearance of the diamond,' he remarked.

'No: but have you a clue?'

'It is the prerogative of the police to cross-question,' he parried, but not repressingly, and he added disarmingly 'I shall be glad if you will tell me anything that your common sense has noticed.'

'I shall be glad to tell you anything with substance in it.'

'You are not free from suspicion.'

'Suspicion has been semaphoring towards me from the beginning. The Indian makes no bones about it.'

'I don't want to have to suspect you unnecessarily.'

'Thank you, kind sir,' I said with a mock curtsey.

'You and Miss Osterley are both in low water financially, *you* are here masquerading as a maid, and you are from Australia, a cool plucky pair of young women who think no more of going to the North Pole or jumping into a military scrap than . . .'

'Must one be a clinging weak-kneed rabbit to be beyond reproach of jewel robberies? Why do you men love to suspect brave decent women when you'll mostly find it is the sexy so-called feminine types that let you down.'

'Women of the most Calvinistic upbringing often do the most lawless things, succumb suddenly to temptation. Miss Osterley is a friend of Lady Tattingwood, and I'd like to stop this thing from going any farther if possible. I want you to help me. I've known women, respectable mothers of families in the old houses, as good as this, to do many worse things than hold on to a gem in hope of a reward for its recovery. If you know of the whereabouts of the gem, there is still time to turn back. Don't be offended! You'd like to save Miss Osterley from trouble, wouldn't you?'

'Chief Inspector Stopworth, if this is a mild form of the Third Degree, you are wasting your time.'

'We always find out in the end. A gem like that could not be disposed of easily.'

'You'll never find that gem about me unless someone hides it there as a way out. Honestly, I don't know where it is now that Percy and Yusuf have both been proved innocent. You surely don't suspect Miss Osterley?'

'It is my business to think no one above suspicion till this is cleared up, but if I trust you, I wonder if you will return the compliment and trust me sufficiently to help – and to clear yourself from any suspicion.'

'I should love to trust you,' I said mockingly.

'I have sometimes found a woman's intuitions as reliable as clairvoyance or psychometry in certain cases. All I ask is that you confide in me, in strict confidence, your suspicions.'

'Suspicions can be very cruel. I am suspected, though innocent. It has cured me of suspecting others.'

'Quite, but I should regard your suspicions as confidences,

would not even take a note of them, and they would be used only if there was reliable evidence.'

I laughed a little, considering the only suspicion that was left me now that Yusuf was reinstated in respectability sounder than my own.

'Tell me what you are keeping back?' he urged suddenly.

'I think we are keeping back the same thing,' I chuckled.

'That cannot be proved unless you tell me what you are keeping back.'

'Very well. The lights were a long time coming on in the cinema hall this evening, considering that you were standing right beside the switch, and I thought you looked a little disarranged as if the burglar might have given you a wipe on the cheek; and you had a tuft of hair sticking up, whereas your head is generally as sleek as a head can be.'

'Thank you,' he said gravely. 'I shall be obliged if you will continue to exercise your unusual powers of observation, and let me know of anything you consider worth reporting.'

I was free. There was nothing more to be done now but to retire for what remained of the night. It was about 2.30, and as we had supped sumptuously, and it was Sunday, anyone who so chose was free to remain undisturbed till luncheon.

I made elaborate preparations for bed. Zarl had not yet come upstairs. An unopened letter was awaiting her on the dressing-table.

It must be borne in mind that we were in a large room adjoining Lady Tattingwood's. We entered from the grand gallery by a door situated a little from the middle of the room. There was a door into Lady Tattingwood's room in the right-hand corner near the windows. The fireplace was in the centre of the opposite wall, and to the left of that, obliquely from Lady Tattingwood's door, was the door into the room occupied by the Chief Inspector. There were noble windows in the outside wall, which was the front of the house.

These windows opened on to a stone gallery or balcony, with steps leading down to the terraces, so I made sure of all the fastenings. We could do without fresh air for a little while. There was a bolt on the door into the Chief Inspector's room so I slipped that into place, but there was no way of locking the door into Lady Tattingwood's apartments. I shoved Zarl's bed farther into the corner, walled by the gallery, opposite the windows, and pulled my stretcher parallel with it.

Zarl entered at this stage. 'What is the matter with you?' she exclaimed. 'Are you a mallee hen making a nest? Let's flop into bed as we are and leave the whole bally turmoil-in-a-thimble about a bit of coloured glass till the morning. I wish I could find the foul thing now and I'd never say a word about it, but keep it for my old age.'

I drew attention to the letter. 'Jimmy's scrawl! Well, that can rest till morning anyhow. One lunatic is enough per hour, and the Elephant Hunter is as cracked as a gridiron.'

'Was he ever known to utter a sound?' I enquired.

'You should have heard him down there now. He feels as I do about the diamond. He says if he could get hold of it he would stick to it till the fuss blows over.'

'Would you say that was more a sign of lunacy than of the average business spirit of the day?'

'If he had stopped there, but he said that if he could get hold of the diamond he could take me for the most astonishing expedition into Central Africa.'

'Well, but you are always talking about expeditions, and inspiring men to them.'

'That would be an expedition with a bull elephant . . . but listen to Jimmy. Percy could write a better letter. "To see you again raises all the old mad longing. You inspire me to great flights, and this is to say ta-ta, as I may take off in a hurry while you are still asleep. Just to ask you to believe in me whatever happens. Whatever the outcome I shall do it for you!"'

'What do you think he means by that?'

'That his top storey is addled . . . dear me, why should men be such awful bores?'

'You deserve it. You bring it on yourself.'

'One must do something to pass the time, and men put up such a bluff of daring and brains that I like to see if they can be diddled – and they all can be – oh, my, I believe I could leave them all behind if I set about it.'

I pulled back the curtains, switched off the lights and tested the possibilities of silhouettes, which are fruitful, as those who lie often awake in the so-called dark, well know. I laid the heavy broom, with which I had threatened Yusuf earlier in the evening, beside my stretcher, and then turned my attention to Percy, who was looking at me over the edge of the waste paper basket.

I was now satisfied that against the windows or the fire, which had lately been refuelled and would burn for several hours, I should have an outline of any movement that might occur in the room, except in Zarl's corner, and I did not expect anything to happen there but Zarl's wholesome and happy capacity to sleep, by which at twenty-six she still looks like eighteen, and, combining maturing mentality with physical youthfulness, promises to be as permanent as Cleopatra.

'I've had so many late nights lately that I am just dizzy with sleep. Do settle down. You are as restful as a box of fleas,' she complained. 'And what are you doing with Percy? My life hereafter with him will be a misery. I have to live with the contumacious little debbil-debbil, and you spoil him.'

I took Percy from his moorings and let him come to bed with me – against the law. Zarl said that firmness was needed lest our infatuation make of us replicas of those poor old potties who go balmy over some mangy cat or dog. Percy, however, was daintier than any cat or dog could ever be, and it was laughable to see him go to bed. No sitting on top of covers or at the foot of the bed for him. With great authority and equal satisfaction he pulled back the sheets and got in. His gurgles of gratification as he snuggled against me, one tiny arm thrown clingingly around my chest, his soft little cheek to mine, were comfort to the saddest soul.

'Now old man, if the Tattingwood ghost walks to-night, I have done my best.' I was guarding against any attempt of Yusuf to abduct him. If we had been given the gem neither Zarl nor I would have parted with Percy. We lacked financial proclivities and were thus saved many temptations.

There was a nervous expectancy in my being to scatter the bouquet of sleep, and Percy, so near to me that I could hear and feel his breathing, also kept me alert, but sleep enfolded the house, a fine deep sleep, as to be expected after such a night on a cold winter Sunday morning in a great country house. The place was soon wrapped in abysmal quiet. There was nothing but the dropping of the coals in the grate. Even I grew drowsy.

CHAPTER 14

I was envying Zarl her sound sleep, when she surprised me by sitting up and slipping noiselessly from her bed. I did not tell her that precautions against waking me were unnecessary because I wished to nurse my drowsiness. She picked up Lord Tattingwood's foot-stool and set it to keep the door ajar, and went out into the gallery as she was, without a dressing gown. She was away so long that I wondered if she were keeping a tryst. I was aroused from a doze by her tapping sharply on the door. She entered with the foot-stool in her hand and expressed annoyance that I did not more expeditiously admit her.

'I saw you placing the foot-stool to keep the door open.

'I was so sleepy I could not have put it in the right place, and the wind from somewhere sucked the door shut.'

'Where in creation have you been all this time?'

'Keeping your appointment with Swith, of course; I couldn't have him disappointed.'

She warmed herself by the fire and shivered so that I cast an eiderdown about her. 'You look as if you had seen the ghost.'

'I did.'

'What was he doing?'

'He was after the blue diamond, I think, but I told him I already had it.'

'What was he like?'

'Exactly like the Elephant Hunter walking in his sleep. The silly ass was in the corridor just near here and was apparently horrified at my immodesty in seeing him.'

'What was he doing?'

'Don't be such a peanut at this time of day! I suppose he was trying to save his life after that filthy lobster, the same as myself, but he was so mid-Victorian that he was shocked to be seen or to see me in my night lingerie, and stalked off like Anthony Comstock.'

'But what would he be doing in this wing? I thought he was a mile away near Swith and Jimmy.'

'Don't be such a goat with a castiron throat – the other queue might have been longer.'

Zarl was cross. I forbore to annoy her further. Mommer Zaltuffrie had earlier expressed her contempt for the scarcity of sanitary accommodation.

I offered to go in search of alcohol or other remedies, but Zarl said she was now quite all right, and snuggled into bed. I turned off the light again and we finally settled down.

I must have been dozing, perhaps had fallen quite asleep – the slightest sound awakens me – and I thought I heard the faint click of a key in the yale lock of the door. I fancied, that I felt rather than saw the door half open, and a form enter. It was wrapped in a sheet or something that rendered it shapeless, but gave an impression of height as it moved somewhere between me and the fireplace. I thought I saw a big arm wave like a scare-crow's, and that something fell with a sharp plunk near where my stretcher had originally been placed. I became helpless with fear. Stories of the ghost had a horrent effect on my hair. I could have sworn to hearing the door click as the apparition retreated. Petrification continued for some moments and then my goose-flesh mentality subsided sufficiently for me to note that Percy had given no grunt of warning. I came to the conclusion that it was a nightmare induced by lobster salad. Either that or Jimmy was acting ghost for Ydonea, and calling on Zarl in the process. I was relieved to find myself alive and well with Percy on my chest. I could hear Zarl's steady breathing near me.

I turned over. Percy scrambled over my head and took up a new position mouth to mouth. I did not approve of it, but the attempt to place him otherwise aroused wild protests likely to result in scratches. Mother Macacus had evidently trained him to sleep in that position so that she could warn him of danger by a mere accentuation of breath.

The next sound thoroughly awakened me. It was the opening of the door from Lady Tattingwood's apartments. Percy did not hear anything. Zarl's regular breathing continued. I added mine, and lay watching between half-closed eyelids. Clarice was recognisable against the windows as she stole across the room obliquely and disappeared in the doorway to Stopworth's room. She was some time softly withdrawing the bolt, but eventually was through to the other side with the door closed and fastened behind her. I sat up quite interested, though, as far as I could gauge, her business with the Chief Inspector could have little to do with the diamond mystery. She too might be suffering from the lobster, but surely would not have put such a strain on romance as to seek the Captain, while women were at hand. I thought I heard a cry. Could she and Stopworth be quarrelling! I got out of bed and went to the door. I touched it, but it did not open. It was heavy and fitted perfectly. I listened for fully five minutes, but could hear no sound of any kind from the room, so crept back to the warmth of Percy, who was sitting up like little Wilhelmine with wonder waiting eyes, and guffing questioningly.

I had scarcely composed myself and Percy, when he warned me by a little guff, no more than a stressed breath, and I saw that the door from Lady Tattingwood's apartments was opening again. A form disguised in some sort of cloth stole towards the fireplace and groped about where Percy had been moored to the coal-scuttle earlier in the evening.

I lifted the heavy broom, and raising myself, struck with all the force I could employ. The implement dropped with a fine felling thud on some part of some person. Whoever it was went down without a cry, but was up again and through the door into the gallery with amazing agility.

Now that the hunt was raised, Percy emitted loud grunts and sprang bang on to Zarl's curly head. That, following the thump of the broom, thoroughly aroused her. She sat up demanding 'Did you fall? Has Percy knocked something down? I'll turn on the light.'

In removal, her bed had been pushed away from the switch,

and I had to grope about for it. When the light came on, Zarl had Percy in her arms, and I crept in beside her shivering from sleeplessness and fatigue.

'Some one has been in the room groping about for Percy, and I lashed out at him with the broom. That was the thump you heard.'

'Let's wake Clarice at once.'

I related in a hurried whisper that Clarice, sometime since, had gone into the Chief Inspector's room.

'Good heavens!' exclaimed Zarl. 'You've been asleep, and then rose up and hit her when she was on the way back.'

This was a disturbing suggestion. We sat up in bed. We looked over the footboard and saw something lying there. It was what the intruder had been wrapped in, a purple silk bed cover.

'Clarice's counterpane!' exclaimed Zarl. 'And you say you hit her with a broom.' The big broom was lying there in plain sight. 'I must say you are a nice one to bring to a house party among the best people! Surely you dropped to what was going on. Poor old Clarice! I hope you missed her. Don't you think that was more likely?'

I began to think it could have been Lady Tattingwood returning, and that she had missed her direction because of the beds being removed. It was a paralysing thought. 'What had we better do? . . . but I still believe that it was Yusuf after Percy. Or it could have been Jimmy and the Elephant Hunter playing ghost. There have been at least two different people in here, or I had a frightful nightmare, that is the only explanation.'

'At anyrate the best line for you to take is that it was Yusuf after Percy. We must do something, no matter how extreme, to save things for poor old Clarice. Let's go shivering in now, and pretend to be frightened, to take the down off the imbroglio. We can hide the counterpane and spirit it back some other time.'

We knocked on Clarice's door. There was no response. Zarl opened the door and peeped in. There was a dim light burning. The bed was empty. 'SSSH! She hasn't returned yet! Cecil is probably massaging the poor thing's bruises. At anyrate I'm glad she has something better than Swithwulf. I wouldn't have had him if he had been dripping with coronets.'

'I should consider Cecil almost sufficient compensation for Swithwulf.'

'Another decent woman ready to go wrong all because of Cecil, but he won't let you make the sacrifice,' said Zarl with a chuckle, climbing back to bed.

I climbed with her. 'Zarl,' I said, and shivered in the recollection, 'I really saw something else before the other two came through, a tall form like a ghost that threw something in the doorway. I heard it fall at the foot of your bed.'

'The bed cover.'

'No, it made a plunk.'

'Lobster salad! I shed mine early.'

'I hope it was that, but if you are game you can get out and see if anything is there. I'm not.'

Zarl said she had squandered her endurance for one night and did not propose to risk pneumonia a second time. 'Get some sleep. We'll need our best working wits to crawl out of that attack upon Clarice. I hope to goodness you did not give her a black eye.'

It was now nearing six o'clock and the idea of a spectral figure seemed to be too much the child of lobster salad to be convincing. I cuddled in beside Zarl and Percy and had a decent sleep.

We awakened about eight o'clock, but as Lady Tattingwood had thoughtfully arranged that no one was to be disturbed that morning until he or she rang, we luxuriated a little longer, and then said we would have a housemaid to clean up the fire and bring more coal.

I sat up and looked at the purple bed quilt again. It was lying flat on an open stretch of carpet, but at one corner was a peak as if a tent peg were underneath. That arm flinging something might have had more substance than a bad dream. I suggested that it might be a good time to get the quilt back to Lady Tattingwood's room, and Zarl agreed. I kept my eyes taut as she withdrew it. There *was* an object sticking in the floor, a dirk or dagger with a hilt like a rapier.

'There, I did hear something!' I exclaimed, pointing.

Zarl stooped and pulled the weapon out of the floor. It

was deeply embedded and required quite a tug. 'Ugh!' she said. 'It has jam or blood or something on it. That brute must have been trying to kill poor little Percy. Oh, do you know, I believe it was that thing they were throwing at the board in the lounge yesterday afternoon. I don't like this kind of a joke. It's carrying realism too far. We must tell Clarice.'

We knocked hurriedly and entered without awaiting response. Lady Tattingwood's bed was still unoccupied. At a casual glance the room seemed exactly as when we last saw it.

'Let's knock up Cecil Stopworth. He's the right person to tell.'

Zarl rapped sharply on his door. There was no response. 'Clarice must still be there. We must give her five minutes to get away.' Zarl had more acquaintance with week-ending among the best people than I had.

In ten minutes we knocked again. Still no reply. No reply from Clarice's room either. We got back to bed for warmth, and discussed the situation. 'If you hit her she is probably with Swithwulf,' said Zarl, now quite serious.

'But surely she did not go to Swithwulf, and risk giving her show away.'

'Clarice isn't one of those recklessly courageous people who has to tell the facts. The weak have a great knack of having things both ways. She could say that she tripped getting out of bed, or anything.'

'But I should think others would be more sympathetic than Swithwulf.'

'Don't you believe it! Clarice's Trustees ensured Swith's overwhelming care, and it's not so abstract as sympathy. The marriage settlement is a masterpiece in its line, I understand. It only holds while Clarice is well and hearty, during her life, and that sort of business. So if she only looks yellow or pink or whatever it is about the gills, Swithy is on the job like a fire squad. He's a wizard nurse too – picked it up soldiering. Clarice has him there, and uses him too. No proud, silent woman scorning his help, about Clarice. And it works. When you see what marriage generally becomes, Clarice's arrangement is rather wizard.'

'Rather, with Cecil as *cher ami*.'

'This one-man-one-woman business in marriage is not the ideal of the smartest people – too much like universal suffrage.'

'How doth Swith take Cecil?'

'As a matter of good form, he ignores it, but it would be all to his good if they would compromise themselves. He is always affable to Cecil. An affair with Cecil, that could be proved, would be security for Swith. If Clarice tried to get a divorce it could be quashed by Swith countering with Cecil as co-re, and the fortune would remain where it is. And there are a couple of other men who would gladly snap up Clarice's soap if she were free – the Elephant Hunter for one.'

'I see,' I said. Zarl had been put in that room because she was a friend whom Clarice trusted, whom anyone could trust both for tact and loyalty, and I, thrusting in as maid, had spoiled things. 'What can we do to mend matters?' I said rather helplessly, and looked out on the park, clear in a crisp frosty morning after a fog-wrapped midnight.

'We must do something. Swith doesn't encourage people who are a menace to Clarice's health.' Zarl rang our bell, and tardily, a house-maid came. Zarl asked her to attend to the fire. We got back to bed. The girl must have been fifteen minutes. As she was withdrawing Zarl instructed her to go to Capt. Stopworth next door and ask him to come to us as soon as possible.

In due time the girl returned with a scuttle of coals, and said no one answered her knocks next door, and that the door was locked. Zarl suggested that the Chief Inspector must have dressed and gone downstairs, and asked the girl to seek him. Later she reported that Chief Inspector Stopworth was not to be found, but that Detective-Constable Manning was in the Servants' Hall. Zarl asked for him and he came in a few minutes.

He rapped with authority on the door in the gallery, and then tried the one leading from our room. Both were locked from the inside. The windows opening on to the outside gallery were also firmly fastened. He went for Detective-Sergeant Beeton, who came with implements, and they forced the door from the gallery.

In company with the police officers, Zarl and I peeped in.

Chief Inspector Stopworth was lying full length on the floor on his back, one arm flung out, the other by his side. His face showed that he was dead.

'Um!' remarked Detective-Sergeant Beeton.

The other man pursed his lips. Zarl and I were sick with horror, too stricken for words.

Newspaper stories of murder run so simply that frequently they fail to interest the outsider. It is a different thing to see the foul thing before one's eyes, to find the remotely considered become reality, to have felt its dread breath as it passed to reduce to ungainly death one who a few hours earlier had been the most commanding personality, the most beautiful being present.

The detectives re-locked and guarded the room till the regular procedure could be observed. The Yard was immediately informed. Lord Tattingwood had to be told.

Zarl and I scuttled back to our room. Zarl tripped over the heavy footstool, and, recovering herself, set it against the door into Stopworth's room as if placing a barrier between us and horror. I don't know if I looked as startled as she did, or as pale. She sat shivering by the fire.

'What are we to do?' she demanded. 'I never thought it would end like this. Shall I have to say that I saw the Elephant Hunter when I was out last night? And he'll say he saw me.'

'You mustn't conceal anything, or you will be an accessory.'

'I'd rather be considered that,' said Zarl, 'than seem to be kicking a man when he is down. What ought I to do?'

'Wait till we find out what the Elephant Hunter says. He may confess his movements. They probably were as innocent as yours.'

'He looked as if he were walking in his sleep.'

'He always looks like that.'

But Zarl when first mentioning him had ridiculed his modest manner upon encountering and being encountered in his night apparel.

CHAPTER 15

Lord Tattingwood was out of bed, but undressed and unshaven. His wife was in his room, wrapped in blankets on a couch. Lord Tattingwood said he had found her half-an-hour since, cold and ill, in his dressing-room. Alarmed by her condition, he wanted to telephone for the doctor at Supersnoring immediately, but Lady Tattingwood had insisted that she was only suffering from colic, which she attributed to the lobster salad. Her husband had administered brandy, which she said gave her instant relief, which endured as long as she remained perfectly still.

She murmured that she wished to be left alone, and Lord Tattingwood emerged to learn of foul murder committed under his roof. Unshaven, in the morning light, he looked old and dissipated, and an even less attractive being than during the previous evening, when he had told the fib about his visit to Percy. But on hearing the state of affairs he took command with that energy and common sense to be expected of an intrepid soldier. His first thought seemed to be for Lady Tattingwood. He said this would be a terrible shock to her, as the Chief Inspector had been one of her patients during the war, and they had been friends and companions ever since. As the doctor had been sent for on the other count, he would let her rest undisturbed as long as possible.

He said he would inform his son, and retreated for that purpose. In a very short time afterwards, he and Cedd, shaven and dressed, were everywhere, directing the household staff, assisting the police and consoling their guests.

The detectives, in collaboration with the local police,

92

proceeded with their scientific routine, taking evidence, searching for clues. The housemaid, who had knocked on Stopworth's door at our behest, was the first to be questioned. I came next. I told of waking from a troubled doze and fancying that I saw a great arm fling something into the room, but this had seemed so fantastic that I attributed it to nightmare and went to sleep again till thoroughly wakened by the entrance of someone disguised in a wrap, whereupon I had struck out with the broom, and the person had scuttled out the door into the gallery. As there had been no light in the gallery I was unable to discern an outline in that direction that would have helped me to identify the intruder.

Zarl corroborated my statement, but omitted to say that she had been out in the night and had seen the Elephant Hunter. She simply testified that she had been awakened by a thump, which I had explained. Neither Zarl nor I wished to bring Lady Tattingwood into it unless necessary.

'Why did you not alarm the household?' the Detective demanded, very naturally.

We said we saw the purple quilt on the floor and were horrified to think that we might have struck our hostess. We immediately sought her in her room but had found it vacant. We then knocked on Capt. Stopworth's door and received no answer, so were in a quandary, but as we saw and heard no one about, we felt that the best thing to do was to return to bed and wait till morning. It was only when we lifted the bed quilt that we found the weapon, and then did arouse the house.

The detective censured Zarl for touching the weapon, though in this instance it did not so much matter. The weapon was readily identified as that with which the man had been playing on the previous afternoon, and showed a medley of fingerprints useless as a clue.

My story of how the dagger came into our room did not ring very well in the circumstances. Zarl and I were asked to remain at hand for the present.

When we were alone, Zarl said that she had not mentioned going out into the corridor during the night and seeing the Elephant Hunter. 'I let it slip, and now I may get into a terrible mess. It's not like a thing I could forget, and I don't know what to do. What should I do?'

'They'll probably question you again and then you could mention that you were out, but just after you went to bed: affect modesty about your errand, and that will cover the thing, I should think.'

'It's not my being out that I mind telling – it's seeing the Elephant Hunter.' Later she said, 'I'm not going to tell that I saw the Elephant Hunter or that I was out of my room at all. If he committed the murder and my withholding the evidence lets him get free, no very great harm will be done, as he'll most likely go back to the Congo and stay there for fear of being found out. Please don't tell a word of this.'

I promised.

Lord Tattingwood could throw no light on the subject. He said, that with a number of his guests, he retired about 3 a.m., and had gone to sleep at once. He was a heavy sleeper and did not hear his wife enter his dressing-room. She had called till she wakened him only about half an hour before Detective-Sergeant Beeton came to him. He slept so heavily that it was always difficult to wake him, and he had heard no sound from the time of his retirement until Lady Tattingwood's call aroused him. He asked the Sergeant to defer questioning Lady Tattingwood till she had recovered from her swoons. He dreaded the effect of breaking the news to her, and preferred to wait till the doctor came.

A roll call of every member of the household – staff, guests and family – showed that two were missing, Yusuf and Jimmy. London was immediately communicated with and the local police set to scour the neighborhood for evidence of the movements of these two men.

No bruise was found on anyone that would tally with my tale of defensive attack, but Yusuf and Jimmy Wengham were missing. A lot seemed to hang on them.

Yusuf had not been seen by anyone after he got out of the car when he returned from the X-Raying.

It was now recalled that Wengham had been in his thick clothes and air helmet when we had departed for the Hospital. He must have changed out of his evening dress after being searched for the blue diamond. This had passed unnoticed as he had come forward offering himself as driver, also he had a mania for air gear and would have worn it to dinner if permissable. He had occupied a small room adjacent to the Elephant Hunter's, in the bachelor wing, in the direction of Lord Tattingwood's apartments, and his bed had not been disturbed at all on Saturday night. The Elephant Hunter had not seen or heard him there.

Ydonea Zaltuffrie's company were all accounted for except Yusuf, and yielded nothing under questioning. The magnates had been undisturbed by eating the lobster salad, a form of cannibalism to which their digestive apparatus was inured. They were intrigued or disconcerted according to their temperaments, and consorted together in the smoking or billiard rooms.

Mammy Lou alone yielded anything of interest. She was too ill to get up, but she was immensely fat and quite forty, and it was unlikely that she could have disappeared with the celerity that I noted in the intruder. She testified that she had eaten all the lobster salad provided for her mistress and some more as well, and after retiring had been taken ill. She had gone out into the corridor of the east wing, where Ydonea was quartered, and at the end of the hall had seen a ghost, and rushed back to her mistress jibbering with terror. She insisted that it was a real ghost, though she saw it only for a moment before it disappeared around a corner. She still shuddered and became unintelligible when questioned, but asserted that the creature had been immense and white, shapeless and awful, and reached nearly to the ceiling.

Ydonea said it was the dream of her life to visit a baronial hall and see a real live ghost, so she had dashed out into the corridor, but could see nothing. She ran to the end where it joined the grand gallery, but the lights there had all been put out, and she returned to deal with her panic-stricken maid. She thought the tale denoted that Mr. Wengham or the Elephant Hunter had been playing a practical joke for her benefit when interrupted by Mammy Lou, and had attached no further importance to it.

My story of the sheeted figure gained a little weight, but Zarl said to me privately that Mammy Lou had seen the Elephant Hunter and her fright had enlarged him to a ghost.

The doctor's evidence, in common language stripped of terms like *rigor mortis* and other technicalities, was that Stopworth had been stabbed in the chest by a sharp pointed instrument, and could have been dead about four or six hours. As indicated by the position of the body the blow had been savage, from a strong arm, from someone as tall as Stopworth himself, and death had followed without a struggle. Stopworth lay where he had fallen, soaked in his blood. He was wearing slippers and a thick dressing gown over his underclothes. By the disposition of a deep, easy chair and the reading lamp he had evidently been writing when disturbed. This was borne out by there being on the floor near to his outflung left hand a fountain pen and a note book. There was a gas fire in the room and this and the reading lamp were both alight when the body was found. Owing to the absence of any evidence of struggle it seemed that the murdered man had been taken unaware, as he was tall and athletic, excelled at tennis and rowing and always kept physically fit.

The position of the lamp threw the door from the gallery in shadow. Anyone rising from the lamp and fire might not at first glance have recognised who was at the door as he opened it. It seemed as if Stopworth had removed his pen to the left hand with the book while he used his right fingers to turn the yale lock.

Considering what had happened before he retired and that he was an alert efficient man, the detectives were of opinion that he would not have gone to the door in such a fashion unless someone on the outside had spoken to him, someone whom he could trust. Therefore the intruder must be someone whose voice was familiar to him, or someone who had been able to imitate the voice of such a person. Nothing had been removed from the room nor from the dead man's belongings so far as expert search could ascertain.

The book in which the Chief Inspector had been writing at the time of his death was the usual professional record of such cases. The events of the evening from the dead man's trained point of view had been written in his small clear hand. It was not a printed diary, but a small ledger with a lock and key, in which he had made his own divisions for the days as he needed them, some small, some larger. Scattered throughout it were pages of shorthand, in neat almost perfect characters; the kind of shorthand learned for keeping a personal private record and never roughened by speed.

Zarl was known to be an authority on shorthand. She had once studied the various systems to find the most easily acquired so that she could be secretary at about three weeks' notice to a great man going to observe sub-arctic growths in the carbuncles of the moose in Alaska, or some other recondite scientific quest. The book was handed to her to discover the system used, as none of the police officers present could decipher it.

Zarl said it was not Pitman, nor Gregg nor Webb. 'Do you know it?' She turned to me. Detective-Sergeant Beeton was not too pleased, but did not like to be curt with Zarl (the famous charm was operating), and with himself watching, I could not very well eat the book, so he submitted. I saw it was the script I use, learned through a correspondence school. The Chief Inspector had evidently taken such a course when he was demobilised and did not know what to do. When I got the slant of the characters I could read them as certainly as much handwriting of the highly educated, but pretended to be boggling so as to learn as much as possible.

'Come!' said the Sergeant. 'You cannot decipher it. We'll send it to Headquarters.'

'I was just beginning to understand. He is explaining that when the lights were switched off at the cinema show the diamond disappeared.'

'I could guess that,' said the man dryly.

'Thank you,' I said, demurely returning the book, which was sent to Headquarters by a motor cycle messenger. I did not confess what I had learned of its contents. The C.I.D. was so efficient that my help was superfluous, and all men prefer people who have less ability than themselves. If I was to be suspected, concealed knowledge rather than intrusiveness would help me more in learning the progress of the case.

My own name and Zarl's occurred in Stopworth's diary. I was commended as being shrewd and observant, quick at deduction and inference, and not easily rattled. Zarl was spoken of as daring and interesting and as one who might know more of the matter than she would divulge. The unfinished pages were in script and in them was the statement that the yellow diamond had also been taken from Stopworth's pocket when the lights went out in the cinema hall; that he had not yet traced it, though E.C.'s evidence as to how certain men were placed when the lights went on, gave him a clue. The chewing gum which the Indian Chauffeur had produced (alleging that he had found it on the under part of the head rest of the tall chair on which Zaltuffrie had been sitting, and from which the Indian said he had taken it upon entering the room after the search had been completed) contained an impression of a diamond. It was likely to be that of the blue diamond, and whoever snatched that had evidently adhered it to the chair with the gum and risked it being there later. The dead man deducted that this could have been Yusuf, or Yusuf might be working with a confederate. The gum had been handled with a handkerchief evidently, so that no impression of fingers was on it. Two people, and probably more, had been needed to pass both the blue diamond and the yellow one through the searching of persons and the room which followed on the alarm being raised. It was possible that the blue diamond had been passed to Yusuf from some person near Zaltuffrie who could have tossed it to the adjoining room while the lights were off and then recovered it while pretending to grovel with E.C. and search for what had flipped from the monkey and which E.C. had alleged was a button. The yellow as well as the blue diamond was missing. Yusuf's every move must be watched. Wengham and Brodribb were also near Zaltuffrie, and Carrington and Osterley. He felt that the diamond had been picked from his pocket by . . .

That was the end.

CHAPTER 16

As soon as the doctor had pronounced the dead man officially to be dead, Lord Tattingwood called him to his wife. He said he had just broken the terrible news to her, and was alarmed by the result. She had fainted dead away, and was too long coming to for his liking.

When she came out of her swoon she asked that Zarl should come to her and remain with her during the doctor's visit. It was to Zarl that she turned and clung rather than to the family connections such as Miss Bitcalf-Spillbeans, who loathed monkeys. I consoled myself with Percy, who was full of capers. Suspicion and danger seemed to have been removed from him, but I was embedded in the terrible drama, one of those to give evidence, one of those receiving censure for what I had omitted to do, and most likely being suspected of what I knew not.

The guests collected in whispering knots and discussed Lady Tattingwood's indisposition. They said the shock of Capt. Stopworth's death had been too much for her, as she had been at one time attached to him. Some of the kinder hoped that Swithwulf would be considerate, said that he owed it to her as she had been so generous with her fortune and so tolerant of his humiliating infidelities. It was admitted that he had risen to the occasion remarkably, with thoughtfulness for all and a dignity that became him, though he looked shocked and worn. 'I could have met this thing better thirty years ago,' he remarked to Zarl.

Zarl reported to me that upon examination the doctor speedily discovered much amiss with Clarice, plus the alleged lobster colic. For one thing her elbow was fractured. The doctor wanted to take her to the Supersnoring Home for Cripples and have it X-Rayed, but her husband said he would take her direct to Wimpole Street, and call in his friend, Sir Philmore Galstone, the distinguished surgeon of Harley Street.

Inspector Frereton from Scotland Yard had arrived during the last half hour to take charge, and he said it was necessary to question her ladyship. As she was so ill and suffering, Lord Tattingwood and Zarl were allowed to remain in the room and help her in any way possible with cushions and draughts of water or sips of brandy.

She said that about an hour after she went to bed, she had been attacked by violent pains. At first she could not even ring her bell or call out, but after a while the pains eased, leaving her so weak that she wished for brandy. She had no spirits in her room but thought that Captain Stopworth would have some. She did not wish to wake Miss Osterley and her companion after the tiring experiences of the night. She thought she heard the breathing of both as she stole across the room and knocked on Capt. Stopworth's door. She expected him to be busy writing up events, but there was no answer to her knock, so concluding that he had retired, she was retracing her steps with the intention of ringing for her maid, when she was attacked in the most violent and astonishing manner and had all she could do to rush through the door into the gallery. She was so terrified that she sped to her husband's protection and reached his dressing-room door. This fortunately was unlocked, as she had sufficient strength only to tumble in.

The Inspector asked if she had cried out or screamed when hit. She said she thought she had, but could not be sure, she was in such a panic, the assault had been so sudden and horrid; she thought it must have come from someone in hiding to steal the monkey on account of the mystery about the gem.

'But if your ladyship thought that, how is it that you did not raise the household after reaching your husband's apartments?'

'Oh, I ran such a long way; I thought I'd drop before

reaching refuge, and I must have fainted inside the door. I have been fainting ever since my husband found me. The pains came on again and I thought I was dying. I was quite helpless. The pains were worse than the clout.'

Lord Tattingwood interposed that she had not been quite coherent when he found her. The Inspector regretted her inability to raise the alarm at the time. She was not reprimanded as I had been. She was seriously ill, and the doctor had to attend her. A trained nurse was summoned from Supersnoring.

Inspector Frereton was cool and smart. Stopworth had been equally cool and smart but mellower through experience, and knew how to hide his official contempt for laymen and suspects. Inspector Frereton put me through a fresh examination.

He asked why had I the broom in readiness. I said, in expectation of an attempt to abstract Percy. I confessed I expected Yusuf, because he averred that Percy had swallowed the missing gem, and further, had been vociferously unsatisfied with the evidence of the X-Rays.

'How did you expect him to get in?'

'I wasn't able to lock Lady Tattingwood's door, and I thought he might steal through that way, that is if she did not lock her door into the gallery; or that he might have secreted himself somewhere in her rooms after returning from the X-Raying, and while we were diverted by supper, and so forth.'

'And how do you account for that dagger being where it was found?'

'I cannot account for it. It was flung by someone who had designs on the life of the monkey or me?'

'And that you suspect is . . .'

'I have nothing but suspicions, very addled suspicions, and suspicions are not evidence.'

'The form that Mammy Lou thought was a ghost was probably Lady Tattingwood running to her husband's protection.'

'I cannot say, but the form that I thought I saw throwing the dagger into my room was much bigger, much taller than Lady Tattingwood.'

'As tall for instance ... can you make a comparison by someone in the house?'

I thought of Jimmy Wengham because he was missing, but I would not say his name seeing how cruel suspicions can be: and he had been near Zarl when the diamond disappeared. Neither would I mention the Elephant Hunter Brodribb because he also had been near Ydonea; nor Lord Tattingwood because it would have been ungracious now that he was vanquished by tribulation. I said, 'It was a form much taller than Yusuf the Indian Chauffeur; I should say that he was as tall as Captain Stopworth himself, or Detective-Sergeant Beeton, or several of the film magnates.'

'Oh! And have you any reason to suspect that anyone has designs on your life?'

'None whatever. Never in my life have I felt that my removal would be of consequence to anyone.'

'No sheet has been found that could have been used by the alleged dagger thrower. All the beds, linen presses, soiled linen baskets and such have been searched.'

'It could have been the sheet that was spread for Percy at dinner. That was large, and Percy dropped some fruit juice on it, and it would be thoroughly crumpled because Mr. Wengham, the airman, wrapped himself in it and said he could act ghost. Later I wrapped myself in it and came to my room while my clothes were being searched for the blue diamond, and later still I put it back in the dining room so that it could be used for Percy again. Find that sheet. It should be easily accounted for by some member of the household staff.'

'Why did you not mention this earlier?'

'It has just occurred to me. I give it for what it is worth.'

'Thank you,' said the man, with a little less asperity. 'And now, you say you were only half-waked by this apparition that threw the dagger.'

'That is so. I thought I had a nightmare or that it was a ghost and I was too scared to get out of bed and see if something had fallen.'

'You were quite awake later when a second person intruded?'

'Quite.'

'And you did not recognise Lady Tattingwood?'

'The intruding figure was swathed in the purple bed cover, which was dropped in flight.'

'You did not see the figure after the counterpane was dropped?'

'No. It had the shadow of the door and the unlighted gallery behind it. I had arranged my bed so that I should have a possible intruder against the light from the windows.'

He inspected the position of the beds now, and as they had been when more or less open to observation during the previous evening. He noted particularly the spot where the dagger had fallen.

'It is lucky for you that you moved your bed.'

I did not divulge what I heard pass between Clarice and her friend during the evening, nor that I had seen her go right into Stopworth's room some time before I struck the intruder in the purple quilt, and had no difficulty in recognising her. I did not believe that she had anything to do with her lover's death. The downward trend and the savage force of the wound that had killed him showed that it could hardly have been inflicted by a woman as weak as Lady Tattingwood, and it certainly could not have been inflicted by anyone as small as Zarl or I unless on a foot-stool.

'The hand that plunged the weapon right through the strong, fit body of such an alert, able man, in his prime, must have been on the arm of a tall, strong, ruthless man,' I said to the Inspector.

'Not necessarily,' he replied, fixing me with a steady gaze. 'The weapon is as sharp as a needle, and found a spot between the Chief's ribs. He had no clothes much to protect him. Any tennis-playing girl could have done it if she were, say, on a step to give her height.'

This was meant to remind me that Zarl and I were both noted for our vigorous serving in tennis. It was such an impertinent suggestion that I determined not to worry Zarl by repeating it.

CHAPTER 17

The doubly stricken Lady Tattingwood grew worse. Sir Philmore Galstone arrived during the morning.

'He's a pretentious old cow,' observed Zarl, 'the kind that isn't worth bowling over. The greatest living scientists don't put on such dog. He cackles like a quack and leaves the real work to the inoffensive little chap from Supersnoring.'

Sir Philmore expressed a desire to inspect the monkey who had opened the campaign, and while he posed before Percy I inspected him. He suggested that Percy would be an acquisition for the Research people.

'Such a fine fat healthy little chap.'

Zarl filliped Sir Philmore's interest by riposting, 'Oh, but Sir Philmore, you'd be infinitely better – not quite so human, but the physical area is larger – quantity.' She said this with her eyes dancing and the famous charm operating so that it was accepted as wit. Sir Philmore however turned with relief to the Supersnoring practitioner who deferred to his great superior as to God. He had an attitude of deference foreign to Zarl's upbringing, and please God, may life never dragoon her into it.

Zarl observed further, in private, 'It's a fine thing he's so full of himself, or he might have been too sticky-beaked about what happened to poor old Clarice; and dragged her little secret of midnight trysts into the witness box.'

Sir Philmore's edict was that she should at once be removed to a private nursing home in Wimpole Street. Dr. Supersnoring deferentially concurred in this opinion, and Sir Philmore

mentioned the names of two other highly successful phys-
icians whom he wished to call in consultation.

'Such a bared-faced waste of decent soapsuds,' said Zarl.

Mommer Zaltuffrie was glad to potter about and talk to
me. 'Everything nowadays has to be made into a publicity
stunt, or it can't be put across. This doctor lord is monkeying
a full-sized one with this poor lady. I used to think once that
lords and lordesses had to be born, but it seems that they
make new ones themselves, and one of them here has been
telling me that a labour politician who ain't a lord himself
can make earls and barons. That's a new one on me, like
hoisting themselves by their own bootstraps, without even
having the bootstraps. It's sure as good as a play in a monkey
house.'

Ydonea offered to convey her hostess to London in her
super Rolls-Royce, but Sir Philmore insisted upon an ambulance. Lord Tattingwood said that his wife was too ill to see
Zarl, but she sent kind messages to the effect that if Zarl
experienced any trouble arising out of the tragedy or had any
need of funds she was to remember that Clarice was her
banker. I was included, most generously, seeing that I was
supposed to have attacked her with a broom.

Lord Tattingwood added a few words of his own. 'We
don't know where a bally mess like this may end, and er,
should er, there, what I damn' well mean is that in case of
bail you are to give my name, and that includes the young
lady acting as your maid. I saw through her from the start,
and had a good joke at her expense when I did not think
things were going to end this way.' He winked slyly at me.

Something of *noblesse oblige* perhaps in that oblique saving
of face.

Zarl thanked him appropriately, and observed later
'Clarice isn't as sick as they are giving out or else Swith is
rising too marvellously to the occasion: true British blue
blood will tell sort of business.'

He did not appear too desperately depressed by the grim
happening within his doors, but then he had earned a V.C.
in the Boer war by standing at the head of a pass and pitch-
forking the enemy over his head with a bayonet, or some
equally highly esteemed military feat. When young he might

have been the hero of women – of those who creep rather than stand erect.

The Coroner arrived, and when he had gone through the regular routine, permitted Lady Tattingwood to be removed to the nursing home. Lord Tattingwood dutifully seated himself beside her in the ambulance and the local doctor sat beside the driver.

Ydonea received permission to take her retinue back to the Ritz; one of her private detectives was to replace Yusuf. There was no evidence to detain any of these people, magnates or menials, but they were instructed to hold themselves in readiness should they be needed at the inquest. Zarl and I had to remain for the present.

Ydonea bade us good-bye in comradely fashion. 'Gee!' she exclaimed, 'Think of an ancestral palace like this putting on such a show! I'll say it's thrilling! It's the first time I've lived a squawkie, and I want to say right now that it licks the whole of creation out of a made-up one, though you two girls have more of a star part than I. I still want to sign Percy up as my leading man. Oh boy! what a play we could make out of this! Just think of the shots they could get right here without any dressing up whatever! Now if you girls are put to any expense I hope you'll let me in on that, and if you want anyone to sit beside you when the trial comes on, Mommer and I will take turns. I don't believe that either of you know any more about the killing of that 'cute policeman than I do myself.'

I was about to plunge in and ask what she meant, when she broke down and wept like a real person, and had to be comforted by her mother and the still shuddering Mammy Lou.

This delayed her departure for some minutes during which Inspector Frereton was called to the telephone. The Constable stood outside the door of the room while the Inspector telephoned, and in a moment came and said Miss Zaltuffrie and her staff would have to delay their departure till further orders. Word went to the waiting troupe. The engines before the ancestral door ceased their purring. Everyone looked towards the film star. She was now to have her turn in the full limelight.

The Inspector had received extracts from the transcription of the dead man's notes, those referring to the disappearance of the yellow diamond, and it became necessary to question Miss Zaltuffrie.

I was first re-questioned as to what I had said to the dead Chief about the position of certain people when the lights went on after Ydonea called out that the blue diamond was missing.

Ydonea, when questioned, said that Wengham, when moving protectively to her, as I had described after the alarm, remarked that he had taken the yellow diamond from the Chief Inspector.

'How did he take it?'

'He did not say. I kinda thought the Inspector must have handed it back for safety.'

'And what did you do with the yellow diamond when Mr. Wengham returned it to you?'

'He slipped its chain over my head.'

'And no one noticed it?'

'It don't seem as if they did.'

'Not even in the search – you were searched?'

'Oh yes, in a sort of way. But Jimmy had put the diamond on upside down and it was not remarked. No one was looking for it anyway. It had not been lost.'

In such a pawnbroker's display, one crown jewel more or less had passed in the glitter.

'And you have the yellow diamond now – only the blue one is missing?'

'Why no! I gave the yellow diamond back to Mr. Wengham.'

'You did! When?'

'When the schlemozzle about the search had died down.'

'Did you ask him to take care of it?'

'No. He said he would keep it safely for the night, that the Chief Inspector himself might be the leader of a gang of diamond thieves, for all he knew. He said he couldn't see for what other purpose a gentleman like Capt. Stopworth would stick to such a cow of a job for so long.'

Sharply questioned as to why she trusted Mr. Wengham more readily than the Chief Inspector, she said that they were

107

all kinda strange to her and not what she had expected in such a royal castle, but she knew Jimmy to be the son of a bishop, who had a brother a lord, as she had heard his popper preach, and she therefore considered he might know what he was talking about and be more honest than a mere policeman.

Ydonea evidently had not fallen under the spell of Cecil Stopworth. She was not frail sexually, therein lay part of her business ability, nor had she been 'raised' to regard the police as incorruptible.

Asked if she had told anyone that Wengham had the yellow diamond, she said no, or she might as well have left it among her other jewels.

The next question was concerning Chief Inspector Stopworth. Had he spoken to her about the yellow diamond and how it was taken from him? Ydonea said she did not mention it to him at all. He was very busy in other ways. She naturally thought Jimmy had just asked Captain Stopworth for the diamond and that he had surrendered it because Jimmy was the son of a bishop and had an uncle a lord, while Captain Stopworth was only a plain clothes detective.

Her explanation was so obviously honest and unaffected that any social criticism implied was unconscious and therefore inoffensive. She further stated that she returned the yellow diamond to Mr. Wengham's keeping just as soon as he and she were free from the search, which was early, as they were among the first attended to.

The entries in the dead man's diary did not come so far as this. It was possible that he had not noted the gem's return to the neck of Ydonea, seeing that it was upside down and that he might never have thought of its being there.

Mommer testified that she noticed the absence of the yellow diamond when she and her daughter were placing the jewels in their strong box, but her daughter had said that Mr. Wengham was keeping it for safety as in such a mix-up the most unlikely person might be in with the crooks.

The Coroner and Inspector withheld censure. Miss Zaltuffrie's attitude to State jewels was so high, wide and careless that it rather took their breath.

'And what do you think of Mr. Wengham's disappearance with your plane now, including the gem?' she was asked.

'I'll say Jimmy is just the craziest thing. It's what makes him so 'cute.'

It was divulged that Wengham had been traced as far as Paris.

He kept Ydonea's Puss Moth at a Club at Hendon, of which he was a member. The machine had been left there on Saturday morning, because there had been a thick fog and he could not fly to Tattingwood as arranged. He had returned to the Club in his car some time during the early hours of Sunday. One attendant heard a car and found Wengham's Austin about eight o'clock. There were several to testify that they had heard a plane leaving long before it was dawn. Wengham's Puss Moth and one of the mechanics employed by the Club were missing on Sunday morning. The tanks had been full and the machine in every way ready for a journey. The fog had lifted about 2 a.m. after a shower, and the moon, a day or two past full, had made good light. Wengham had left Paris before he could be apprehended, but the mechanic was on the way back.

Wengham had been quite open about his movements in Paris where he was a familiar figure in aeronautical circles, both on account of his own achievements, and lately as Ydonea's pilot. His papers were in order on account of his frequent crossings. He had re-fuelled, had his machine brought up to the top screech, seemed to have plenty of funds and said he was out to make a new world record in flying.

Telegraphs, cables and air stations were buzzing with messages about him, and as a Puss Moth in full crow is not so inconspicious as a Baby Austin it was expected that he would be speedily intercepted.

Ydonea produced a crumpled note in Jimmy's scrawl in which he expressed himself in the same terms as to Zarl. 'Jimmy never had any originality, that's what dishes him in the heiress marriage market,' Zarl said later. This letter relieved her of any necessity to divulge the note which Jimmy had left her. 'He apparently leaves these chits about with the prodigality of a lady oyster.'

'This note is kind of personal,' said Mommer, 'and doesn't amount to a hill of beans, but I tell daughter she had best not keep anything back in a case like this.'

Jimmy implored Ydonea to think kindly of him, 'and when I make a world record, I'll lay it and myself before you, Baby Doll, for further orders.'

Asked what she took that to mean, she said it sounded as if he was proposing. She generously expressed her belief that Mr. Wengham would be able to account for his actions and would safely keep the diamond for her. She did not attach any particular importance to his using her plane: he was permitted to use it as his own, and had done so several times before.

The grave officials questioning her realised that she had a different point of view from her interlocutors, also she was staggeringly beautiful and young, and the glamour of lime-light and millions enwrapped her. She was permitted to go until the resumption of the inquest.

The date for this was not yet stated.

As the owner of plane and jewel thus gave Jimmy a charter, the police could only act accordingly. As Ydonea testified that Jimmy had the diamond all the time, and as the dead man's diary also stated that the gem had gone from him early in the evening, it seemed to remove any motive on Jimmy's part for putting Stopworth out of existence. Nevertheless efforts to trace him were not relaxed. The blue diamond was not accounted for.

Brodribb, the Elephant Hunter, was asked to remain at hand, but that we did not know till later, so thick was the velvet of C.I.D. manners in conducting their business. He also said voluntarily that he had been out during the night but had seen no one. But he continued to stalk Zarl and fix his petrified stare upon her till she confessed that her nerve would break under the strain.

The terrible day wore on.

Miss Zaltuffrie, reinstated at the Ritz, refused herself to friends and reporters alike. No one could penetrate to her presence. She, who had been flamboyant about publicity, was now acting in an exemplary manner, which surprised and pleased the C.I.D.

Reporters stormed Tattingwood Hall and were met with dignity and impregnable courtesy, first by the butler who passed them on to Cedd — supported nobly by the Elephant

Hunter, whose taciturnity was a refuge. Thus they reached a member of the C.I.D. who said that the police were following several clues. No arrests had been made but a number of persons were under observation.

Zarl was allowed to telephone Mme Mabelle, who said we were just as well where we were for the time, well-guarded from reporters and painful publicity. Cedd had removed us from the tragic wing to a room next to his dressing-room so that we should not feel nervous or lonely.

Cedd was so soothing that I suggested that Zarl should lead him over the brink of matrimony, but Zarl said that two red heads might be a conflagration, that she abominated to be soothed, that what she sought was stimulation, that she would rather be marooned at Russkoye Ustye on the Indigirka with one of her scientists than drop into Ydonea's itinerary.

'But your sorties to Allaikha or the Lena would be immense film stuff. The world is panting for it.'

'But the film concoctors are not. Cedd and his putrid little cliques boost each other as innovators but not one of them has been off the pavements, or farther than a Franch Plage. They cannot see beyond an arc light. But I'll let Cedd sit on the hob and simmer in his own sentimentality for the present – he might prove a useful contraption in this mix-up.'

My functioning as Zarl's maid had broken down. The position had been reversed. She was now my companion, a plucky one that would not leave me. Most of the other guests left on Sunday afternoon and Zarl suggested to Cedd that it would be livelier if we all ate together after that. We were a party of Cedd, the Elephant Hunter, Inspector Frereton, Zarl, myself and one or two left-overs, including Miss Bitcalf-Spillbeans, who considered Percy the source of all the trouble.

When we met for dinner, the Inspector said to me again that the sheet could not be found. The butler said it had been left in the dining hall by Mr. Wengham and the other gentleman who had been playing with it. The housekeeper and housemaids could not account for it.

'It has evidently been carried out of the house by some person,' said the Inspector.

'Or burned. Have you examined all the ashes taken from the fireplaces?'

'Naturally,' he remarked with a cold glance.

Later we learned that Cedd Spillbeans had also been abroad during the night. When about to retire at 3.50 or a little later, he smelt something burning but could not trace the source. The odour was strongest in the corner of the gallery and corridor towards Lady Tattingwood's apartments. The smell of cabbage or other powerful substances often came up from the kitchen by some uncontrollable current. He therefore went down to the kitchen and found a half-burned tea-towel in the ashpan of the range and came to the conclusion that the smell had penetrated upstairs from this.

A few remnants of linen threads had been found among the ashes, but the fireplace from which they had come could not be decided. Other than the great lounge, drawing room and dining hall, the rooms where coal fires had been burning were Ydonea's, Zarl's and mine, the Elephant Hunter's, the housekeeper's and Lord Tattingwood's. I was thankful I was not a tall woman, though a woman of any size can be accessory to the fact of any crime.

The day wore to its close. We were all thankful to see it go. Late on Sunday night there was still no trace of Yusuf. No similar person had been seen at any railway station within a wide radius or noted walking on the roads or by-paths. He seemed to have magically disappeared. He was missing from his lodgings. Such a disappearance indicated that he must have dependable and clever friends.

Percy Macacus Rhesus y Osterley was our diversion. He was enjoying his week-end and eating his fill of grapes, supplied by his friend and patron the butler. He liked dancing before the splendid mirrors, and rolling on the rugs before the big fires – little exile from glorious African sunshine.

The Police were reticent. The dead man had always been secretive about clues in his spectacular cases, and the chief man detailed on his murder was following similar methods.

Certain of the newspapers made harvest of the juxtaposition of the airman son of the aged Bishop of Donchester, the disappearance of the Puss Moth of the fabulously lovely film star, and a cruel murder at such a seat as Tattingwood Hall.

The Bishop had haystacks of spiritual courage, and sought Ydonea, who earned his commendation and affection by her attitude. She said she was sure Jimmy would be able to clear himself. To fly off like that was the kind of crazy thing he would do, but there was no harm in him, and she had nothing to say further than that she had a great regard for Mr. Wengham, who was just one of the 'cutest English boys she had ever seen.

Asked if she would accept Mr. Wengham's offer of marriage (Jimmy's lady-oyster chit had assumed dignity under reportorial pressure), she said she just didn't know; and the Bishop said he would be happy to have such an honest and unspoiled young girl for his son's bride.

Mommer was understood to say 'There are sacks full of more important folks waiting to marry daughter if she ever got time to think of such business.'

Zarl said the best publicity stunt Ydonea could now throw would be to marry the Bish. – that he was just about ripe enough in senility for such a step, and that green or ripe it was all one to men in that department.'

When asked to elucidate whether she meant sex or senility she said that they were indivisible in men, but acted conversely.

CHAPTER 18

On Monday morning a telegram was delivered for Ydonea, at Tattingwood Hall, and as it came through the local office there was no difficulty about its contents.

> TRUST ME AND HELP ME STOP TAKING YOUR MONETARY
> HELP AND PLANE FOR RECORD MAKING WORLD FLIGHT
> STOP DECIDED SUDDENLY TO SNATCH OPPORTUNITY AHEAD
> OF CROWD STOP FULL EXPLANATION LATER STOP
> DIAMOND SAFE YOUR OWN JIMMY.

This history of this message, as compiled by the police, was that it had been found on the table in the Club smoking-room with five shillings and the instruction, 'Don't send till after 8 p.m. Sunday so as not to disturb household.' The message had lain around unnoticed till Sunday evening, which accounted for the delay. The police naturally had been informed as soon as it was found, but it added nothing to Jimmy's chit of proposal.

Jimmy was still at large, but the mechanic who accompanied him as far as Paris had been taken to Scotland Yard to give his version, which could now be made public. He deposed that he slept on the Club premises and had been wakened by Mr. Wengham between two and three o'clock on Sunday morning. This brought great relief to the Bishop. Substantiated, it would be an alibi for his son.

The inquest proceeded on Tuesday afternoon.

Old ground was reharrowed but no important new facts came to light, with one exception, important to those implicated. Other witnesses were found to support the mechanic (who had flown to Paris with Wengham) about the hour of the airman's arrival at the Air Club on Sunday morning. No cross-questioning could shake the fact that this had been between two and three o'clock. Tattingwood was about fifty miles from London. The hour of our departure from Tattingwood to be X-Rayed – when Wengham was last seen – was midnight, so he must have taken his car out under cover of the general commotion and come straight on to London without stopping. Indeed, a local policeman testified that Mr. Wengham had followed our car, having remarked that he would escort us.

An ancient name was thus cleared. Ydonea let herself go in interviews to help the Bishop about Jimmy, and also, the censorious suspected, because she had the habit of publicity. But Zarl said it was partly that Ydonea had the hardiness and simplicity of an aspidistra in her freedom from any need for privacy. She was of the school to whom privacy is concealment, and what should any decent person have to conceal!

The gentle white-haired old Bishop appeared to me an incongruous parent for Jimmy, but Zarl said 'Not at all, among the best people he is suspiciously circumstantial.'

Ydonea said, 'I'll say he's a sweet fatherly old dear.' He became her friend and invited her to be his guest at Donchester.

But Zarl said 'I'll bet you a new pair of stockings to replace those holed by Percy, that she'll marry the Bish. if her publicity dries up.'

It became known from one end of the world to the other that Ydonea and Jimmy had frequently discussed such a flight. It was to have been a secret, but Ydonea had not expected it to be quite so sudden as this. She was proud to have her machine used by such a gallant airman in setting up a world record, and hoped it would be across the Atlantic to her own beloved country. She was quite satisfied with the mention of the diamond being safe with Jimmy. He was using it as a mascot and she hoped it would bring him great luck.

Yusuf could not be traced. There was nothing but slight circumstantial evidence to connect him with the murder. It was surmised that as soon as he heard of it he might have

been terrified of being connected with it because of his eager-
ness about the diamond. It was thought that some of his
countrymen must have aided him to get out of the country
on a substituted permit as a lascar or waiter on a ship going
to the East.

We saw that the police kept clues to themselves more
carefully than is generally credited by the readers of the
sensational press. Some of the evening papers named had
already solved the case. To them it was plain that Yusuf had
escaped with the blue diamond. He had spirited it from the
bracelet after turning off the lights, and placed it in the
chewing gum on the back of Ydonea's chair. The dead man
had suspected this. He had found the diamond himself but
being a secretive worker kept this to himself, the better to
apprehend the thief and his confederates. Yusuf, according
to the evidence at the inquest, had rushed in and found the
chewing-gum as soon as the Cinema Hall was open after the
search. He announced it only because the diamond had
already been taken from it. He knew that Stopworth had the
diamond and had stabbed him in the dead of night and
escaped. The sentimental and superstitious public were sure
that that diamond had gone back to the head of some joss
in India who was worshipped by the subjects of the unnamed
Maharajah. The lay notion of oriental abilities was so exag-
gerated that there was no magic beyond Yusuf.

The Elephant Hunter too was suspect by this audience.
That he had been chewing gum was conclusive to them, and
his exploits in the Congo among savages endued him with
black magic only slightly below Yusuf's. He was the
accomplice of Yusuf, according to the amateur detectives,
and Yusuf had been false to the partnership and got away
with the diamond. Some shuddered and said they would not
have such an unlucky object. Osterley and Carrington were
also not free from suspicion. Carrington's masquerading
looked very fishy.

Ydonea announced that she wished no money to be wasted
or lives to be risked in chasing the diamond.

The Underwriters responsible were not so indifferent and
a reward of two thousand pounds or ten thousand dollars,

was offered for the return of the gem. The C.I.D. expected results from this through the gangsters.

Lady Tattingwood was dangerously ill in a West End nursing home and unable to appear at the inquest, but her depositions were taken. There was some danger with her heart, aggravated by the shock of being attacked and that of hearing of the murder of her friend.

Examination of his effects exposed Stopworth's romance to the police, but if the experts considered that it had any bearing on the murder, they did not divulge it, and the facts were partially suppressed. Lady Tattingwood's letters were found in the dead man's pocket, but they were of ancient date and there was no shred of evidence that Stopworth had ever used them to embarrass the writer. Lady Tattingwood, questioned, said that he had brought them, at her request so that she could destroy them, but there had been no opportunity of a moment of privacy.

Lord Tattingwood, cross-questioned, said that he knew of the old attachment between his wife and Stopworth and had respected their later friendship.

Seeing that this romance was gone for ever, and in view of the fact that Lady Tattingwood might recover and jog along with her husband, the authorities were discreet in handling these facts. Documents concerning Stopworth's daughter Denise were pigeonholed in case of need.

Swithwulf was acting commendably and spent a great deal of time sitting by his wife's bedside. He took up residence at one of his Clubs to be near her.

The weak spot in Lady Tattingwood's story of going to Stopworth's room for brandy, when it was well known that he never touched alcohol in any form, was ignored by the police. Evidence pointed to a more gallant reason for her visit. The allegation of colic had faded in the stress of circumstances, Lady Tattingwood's injuries were officially attributed to the blow attributed in turn to the broom wielded by me.

My story of how the dagger came into the bedroom occupied by Zarl and me, and which was corroborated by Mammy Lou in so far as that a tall, sheeted figure had been abroad that night, had to be accepted for what it was worth.

The Elephant Hunter had not confessed to being in Stopworth's wing. 'I shall keep quiet for ever now,' said Zarl. 'Even if he committed the murder, it's none of my business. They rather suspect you and me, so let them get on with it.'

A verdict of wilful murder was returned, against some person or persons unknown.

CHAPTER 19

When Zarl and I returned to town we found among our mail an envelope addressed in Jimmy's hand from Paris. It contained a scrawled line: 'Mum is the word. MUM.'

'What does he mean by that?' I asked.

'That mum is the word – *silence*.'

'For him or for you?

'For us both, apparently. Well, it's a hygienic recipe in any case, and I'll certainly follow it.'

On careful examination we felt sure that all our mail had been opened, also that our premises had been thoroughly searched.

'I told you they suspected you and me,' said Zarl indignantly. 'I'm ever so glad I never told them about the Elephant Hunter. If I found out the whole thing I should not tell them now. I'd fling the gem down the drain if I found it, and hide the murderer. That Frereton tried to be gallant to me. I suppose he thinks he can infatuate me and discover something. Well, I shall make him in earnest. It won't be hard.'

'Perhaps he is one of those men like Stopworth that has no weakness for women.'

'A fireproof man has not yet been littered.'

'Women are the same . . .'

'Oh no, they are not. Nothing can seduce a really continent woman, but there are no continent men – *de fond en comble*.'

Zarl was so indignant with Inspector Frereton's gallant attitude towards her that I expected a tense experience for him.

We were all back in our usual habitats. Zarl and I had

been so near the noxious breath of the dragon murder that we were depressed. A salutary period of business activity followed to normalise us.

Ydonea had set her heart on Percy. If she had had her way, the public would soon have been clamouring for a film of him, but Zarl was indifferent. She said the possession of Percy was being vulgarised and made a burden. Ydonea placed her hopes on me as his honorary mahout. She offered me publicity work and as I was in low water I could not refuse such a windfall. Ydonea was a wonderful subject. If not occupied with starring she would have made a successful publicity stuntist. Her mind worked on advertisement. Her beauty gave her entry to the film world and she kept a position by publicity. Knowing what the supposedly great artists resort to in advertisement to keep afloat in the moving picture cataract, one respected Ydonea's astute reading of the business.

Physically she was more beautiful than a young lady can be, but she lacked Zarl's power to enchant. Her beauty was so dazzling to behold that it gave one a sense of indecency. Her colouring and features were startling but Zarl had the more allure. She had the seduction of personality that remains like the memory of an exquisite perfume.

I wished I could have Ydonea's appearance for six months as an adventure, but Zarl said. 'It's only a *cul de sac*; people have to turn round and retrace their footsteps.'

'So have they from you,' I contended.

'But I let them prance along the parapet till they're quite dizzy. A very different effect.'

As Ydonea expressed it, she was nix on the murder mystery, but played up the gallant and mysterious airman ranging the universe with her yellow diamond for mascot. She accepted the Bishop's invitation to visit him, and was a country and cathedral town sensation. Cedd managed to kite after her and there was projected a film in which the famous Percy was to co-star with her.

My title of 'publicity' included companion and coolie to Percy, as Zarl would not trust her little friend unprotected with such a collection of oddments. There were many delays. There was the world financial paralysis to contend with, for one. The film magnates were at their wit's end, which Zarl said was not an extensive *cul de sac*. They said that the public was sick of smut and sensationalism. The rage for platinum blondes was quickly dying down. Ydonea persisted that a film with a lead for herself and quite a prolonged part for Percy would be a riot. The drawing power of Percy seemed to give grounds for this idea, but she had much to contend against. Cedd was non-plussed by Percy as a star. He would fit into none of the films he had in mind. It became clear by some inexorable mathematics that an author was necessary. There was a project to buy the name of a big one and hire a continuity expert to set up something in it, but big names are not made by such acceptances, and none was procurable. The matter hung in the air.

We seized the opportunity of directing attention to Percy's own business, which was Madame Mabelle's establishment on Loane Street, were he had a comfortable apartment during the day. Ydonea came there for gowns, all for the wooing of Percy, and Madame and Zarl had such a boom that they could scarcely contend with it in either of their departments, started on high class lines to serve the needs of women. But that is another story.

A day or two after the inquest we had had our first private call from Inspector Frereton, a most presentable young man but not so handsome nor so fascinating as his murdered Chief. It was doubtful if his antecedents were so far up the social ladder as Stopworth's had been, but it was Frereton's preoccupation to give the impression that they were.

'Are you going to accept him as a friend?' I asked Zarl.

'I want to find out what he wants. I think the noble gentleman suspects one or both of us about the diamond, and he thinks I'm the weak woman who will become confidential through his charms. It is a game that two can play at.'

'Yes, and having regard to what you said of men, I know who will win the game, but it will be as deadly a bore as a game of Patience to me.'

It was intensely interesting to observe Zarl's technique. In a matter of days the Inspector was so efflorescent that the flat was littered with chocolate boxes and wilting flowers. The Inspector was not original in gallantry and he did not wade far enough into the syrtis of *amour* entirely to put away the role of sleuth.

'The Tattingwood case shows me that the principal reason why so many criminals are caught is (1) the inferior quality of the headpieces used, and (2) the rarity of the ability to keep silence, and this cuts both ways,' said Zarl, 'And I'm sick of Frereton and shall take a day at home presently to think up a way of getting rid of him. There are gruesome tales of detectives stepping upwards on the misplaced confidences of women. I'd despise him if he did not hang on to his profession, but I loathe him more that he should have an ulterior motive in his prancing on the parapet.'

'Let him simmer on the hob without boiling over,' I suggested. 'Very likely I am the one he suspects as thief of the diamond or accessory to the murder of Stopworth, and we'll never know the end of the story unless we keep in touch with someone on the inside.'

So he was allowed to remain a little longer to talk 'shop' and spread himself as men will to impress a siren with Zarl's gift of listening. There was also mine, and added thereto a turn for cross-questioning under the cover of feminine ignorance and inconsequence. Many of the cases cited by the Inspector to illustrate the prowess of his colleagues seemed ill-chosen to Zarl and me. They proved to us that the marvellous *coups* in recovering gems depended on the burglaries being committed by well-known criminals. In the case of a crime committed sporadically, the mystery could easily remain unsolved. The many unsolved murders proved this and gave rise to Zarl's observation on the quality of the headpieces used on both sides of the chase.

I wished on the fatal Sunday morning, that I could have been as free and as vested in authority as the detectives to wander about the place and observe, but I had been ignominiously detained. Now, without material evidence, I had only my mind to poke into crannies, but that, as Zarl remarked, was an original and independent apparatus. My mind clung teasingly around the movement in Zarl's room on the fatal morning, and returned again and again to my supposed attack upon Lady Tattingwood. Everyone, even Zarl, believed that I had dozed and then started up to give Lady Tattingwood a crack on her return from knocking on Stopworth's door, but I knew differently. Had I walloped Lady Tattingwood on her return, her right arm would have received the blow. It was her left elbow that was injured. Further, to be in such a mess it must have been raised to some angle, say that of defence, which she, taken unaware, would not have assumed. I could not have hit an elbow in its natural position as she walked across the room. Even fear and pain, it seemed to me, would have been insufficient to lift a woman of fifty, rather frail physically, from the floor, and enable her to turn and scurry out the door as quickly as the person I had knocked down. That figure had been facing the gallery door, he was not with his back to it, as Lady Tattingwood would have been, according to her testimony.

She went right into Stopworth's room and drew the bolt after her. I had not insisted upon the fact. I would not be treacherous to a woman in whose house I was lodged in equivocal circumstances. This might be helping a murderer, but the moment for speaking was long past. I must certainly wait until Clarice was able to defend herself.

My first impression was right. It was Yusuf I had struck. It was he who had left the purple quilt behind in his flight. He had come for Percy, believing, in spite of X-Ray evidence, that he had swallowed the diamond. This suggested that Yusuf himself had not procured the blue diamond.

Where was it? Who had it?

If Ydonea had taken it from the bracelet herself, or with the aid of the absent Wengham, for a publicity stunt, the act would operate detrimentally when followed by the loss of a gallant officer's life in pursuance of his duty. In such a case I believed Ydonea capable of throwing the infernal diamond somewhere into the shrubbery or Park where it might lie hidden for a generation, or never be found. Money had come to her so easily that she lacked financial proportion, but she had perception approaching genius for what was popularising publicity or the reverse.

The reward offered had produced nothing, as we knew through Inspector Frereton. There was another possibility.

The doctor at the Supersnoring Home for Cripples had given Zarl a set of the X-Ray photographs. I studied them anew with an idea in mind. Percy had been so lively on that occasion that it had taken both Zarl and me to get him into focus without rough methods. There were fine studies of his head, taken specially to discover if anything was in his pouch. Quite unnecessary, as he permitted Zarl to forage in his pouches as if they were her own. Grapes had been used to bribe him. He was so stuffed with grapes that he had to take one from his mouth to ease pressure and hold it in his hand, and I had held the hand to steady him.

When Zarl came home I locked the door against curious ears and told her that perhaps after all Percy had picked the diamond from the bracelet and had retained it in his pouches for some time before swallowing it, and it was possible that it was still embedded in his intestines. It would clear up one end of the thing to find it, to say nothing of the financial status of the diamond.

'But it would have reappeared ages ago,' said Zarl.

'What things should do and what they do are often wide apart.' I adduced the case of an infant relative who once swallowed a button which should have reappeared in two or three days but which took a holiday of a fortnight and then came to light without harm to the infant or itself.

'There are always exceptions,' admitted Zarl. 'The lives of scientists all remind us that this decade's data is mostly disproved by the next.'

'Well, not a murmur even to ourselves, or Percy would be in danger again.'

'Rather, and *mum* is the word, as Jimmy wrote, though I've never found anyone but myself strong enough to keep a secret.'

Zarl said she would study the photographs that evening to see if there were any grounds for my idea. 'I don't want that foul stone ruining Percy's cog wheels. It would be a relief to be convincingly rid of it at last.'

I had an evening engagement and when I returned, Zarl's light was out. In the morning she informed me that she was not going to business, as she wanted a rest. I asked was there anything I could do for her such as taking charge of Percy for the day, but she said she felt a bit hooey and would like his company, and I went off to Fleet Street leaving her alone.

She had quite recovered when I returned during the early evening. She said she had studied the photographs and saw what I meant. She believed it was just possible that the gem might still be in Percy, and with locked door and in low voices, we discussed the situation. It was necessary to act at once as if the gem appeared no one would believe that Percy had retained it so long.

Zarl ruled out the doctor at Supersnoring. He was kind, accessible, had a fine apparatus and was already interested in Percy, but he was a sociable man and likely to be a blatherer. Desire for self-importance makes it difficult for what is called the normal being to keep silent about anything interesting. Zarl chose Dr. Woodruff of Wigmore Street, known to the world as a martyr to science, not only a great X-Ray expert, but a man of unblemished record.

Zarl insisted by telephone upon Dr. Woodruff receiving us. She did not want the reappearance of the diamond to be a premature birth *sans accoucheur* and other substantial witnesses of its authenticity.

'It may have gone already,' she said. 'Twenty thousand pounds – how much is it worth? No one will ever believe us. We'll just have to live it down.'

CHAPTER 20

We were speedily in Dr. Woodruff's waiting-room, and about twenty minutes later were ushered into his presence, the famous Percy 'lepping' in every direction till Zarl put him competently under her arm and hissed a word into his froward ear.

The doctor rarely read newspapers and so had heard nothing but an echo of the Tattingwood tragedy. The story was told as briefly as possible.

'And what is it you want me to do?' the doctor asked with the direct simplicity of a great man.

'Will you please X-Ray Percy again and see if the diamond is not in him after all, and if it is, will you keep him under observation till it re-appears?'

'But my dear young ladies, what could I do with a mercurial creature like that? He would be more comfortable with you.'

'My friend will stay too,' Zarl said.

I hastened to add, 'Yes. Could you not have me shut in some hospital cell with him to show all was fair and above board? It must be a secret or his life would be in danger; my life would be in danger too; it has been already.'

The doctor, not being avaricious, and knowing little of gems, was as innocent as I had been before I went to Tattingwood Hall. He believed in the honesty of people. Zarl had to convince him of the condition of the average mentality where a famous gem was concerned.

Zarl showed him the X-Ray photographs and stated her belief in the possibility of the gem having escaped the rays because Percy could have taken it from his pouch while I was

126

steadying him. Zarl had not had him to herself for a moment after the cry of his being the thief was raised, and did not suggest examination of his pouch lest some large rough finger should wound him. It had not occurred to others to search him, or else ignorance of his pouch, or fear of monkeys had deterred them. The Elephant Hunter, who knew monkeys, had retained his usual silence. Jimmy Wengham also had said nothing. Zarl pointed out that while Percy's head and neck were being rayed, one of his hands had been in mine, and one plate stopped just short of this.

'Well, just come through here,' said the great man. 'We'll photograph him first and the next step can follow.'

Dr. Woodruff had the charmed way with animals. Percy liked him and tried to chaw a button off his shirt, and then danced on his knee till the doctor gurgled with delight. He was not afraid of Percy's finger nails nor that he was vicious.

'He's a great pet, isn't he, and magnificently groomed and healthy.'

Zarl lent him her hand mirror, and he tried to get at the fellow in its depths, who always eluded him. As he held the glass above his head with both hands it placed his engine department in an excellent position to be photographed.

The result showed a small solid substance within, which the doctor admitted could be a gem. Zarl and I were sure.

The doctor said 'Why not keep the little gentleman under close surveillance and return the gem to its owner as soon as possible?' But Zarl pled for Percy's protection on the grounds that a life had already been lost, and other people tryingly suspected. The matter had to be carried through in a manner above reproach.

The doctor plucked his beard and pondered a few moments till light came to him. 'I'll ask my wife. She will help us.'

Mrs. Woodruff came upon request, and her husband asked us to go with her and make our own explanation. She was one of those wonderful helpmeets that great men occasionally acquire, though rarely through their own perspicuity.

She listened to Zarl, putting an intelligent question now and again and then said she would keep Percy and me with her till all was well. She realised at once that for such a frail little creature to carry a gem worth twenty thousand pounds was dangerous in several ways.

Mrs. Woodruff made it as simple and pleasant as a week-end visit, and both she and the doctor became fast friends with their fascinating simian guest. The doctor photographed him each morning to ascertain whether the object had moved or had become embedded. Progress was eventually hastened.

Towards the close of the third day the Doctor, Mrs. Woodruff and I were on the way to New Scotland Yard with the gem in a pill box in Mrs. Woodruff's handbag, and Percy complacently snoozing in my arms. We reported to Inspector Frereton, who still had the case in hand. He was not at all cordial to me. He said it was incredible that the gem could have been so long retained by Percy. He also said we had been a long time coming forward with this idea. I said I had not looked at the photographs again till recently.

He acted as though he suspected me of purloining the gem in the first instance, and retaining possession through the various searchings by the aid of some accomplice for the sake of the reward, and of later giving it to Percy to swallow as the most plausible way out. It was now that I was glad that Zarl had left him to stew on the hobs of *amour*.

The protection of a man of Dr. Woodruff's standing was also a great help in softening insults to me. We now learned that Ydonea had privately offered a big reward, but the pawn shops had been searched in vain. The diamond was so notable that it would have had to be hidden for years or cut into smaller gems.

Neither Zarl nor I would touch a penny of the rewards. Money in relation to the whole business revolted us as sordid. The Doctor would accept no fee for his professional services, and to entertain Percy and his 'coolie' was Mrs. Woodruff's contribution towards unravelling a mystery. Had we taken the reward it would have proved Yusuf's accusations. As it was, there was plenty of gossip going the rounds in Mack's Bar and more pretentious Clubs and after-theatre haunts to the effect that the whole diamond disappearance was an impudent advertising coup, but it did our business no harm.

We lost no friends by the affair and Zarl said that as for others, they were such a mouldy collection of oddments that she was indifferent to their opinion. Ydonea remained unwithered by any of these blasts. She was a product of the decade and not lightly to be robbed of such magnificent publicity. She was photographed a hundred times with Percy Macacus Rhesus y Osterley, she wearing the notorious diamond in a new setting, or allowing Percy to hold it. She made a personal appearance at the new Doges Palace Cinema House in the West End with Percy, charging an exorbitant sum for this, and paying Percy a handsome salary. She drove through the streets in her limousine with him peeping out the window till the police had to forbid her progress because of difficulties with the traffic.

To compensate Cedd Spillbeans for the way Percy had interrupted his film premier, on which he had placed such high hopes, I got him into the picture too. He said it helped him beyond belief, though it rather disgusted him and was against his County grain, but he had to take the trade on its own tide and leave reform alone for the present.

Upon seeing the crowds that Percy collected every time he walked abroad, he came to the idea of composing a vehicle for him. He visited Zarl's flat, ostensibly to study Percy, but on nights that I was alone he gave very little time to this research. To steady Percy he had an unbreakable mirror, and looking in this he would moan and moan, distracting us from conversation and distressing me so that I folded him in my arms and comforted him, but Zarl said 'Tush Percy, be a man! We all have to endure our faces without such self-commiseration and you must bear up likewise.'

Cedd, colliding with Inspector Frereton, was indignant that he should call on Zarl with such social assurance. 'The fellow is a policeman, not a gentleman!' he remarked with hauteur, but Zarl said that it was a matter of opinion when a gentleman was not a policeman, and *vice versa*.

Cedd wanted to know what she meant, but Zarl said it was obvious to any gentleman, even a police one. Cedd then warned her against bolshevism and 'all that putrid equality rot.'

Zarl pointed out that equality with Inspector Frereton would be exceedingly difficult to attain – physically. He is very well set-up, and Cedd rather scrawny, like the foreign caricatures of an Englishman.

The champagne-bubble expression and effect of Zarl's coquetry hastened Cedd to apologize, by attributing his possessiveness to his ardent passion for her. He proposed once again. Zarl said she had an aversion to marriage as being ruinous of the ecstatic quality of love.

Cedd was so sprung with her allure, and his sense of humour so warped by sentimentality, that he said 'Real love should stand hard wear and tear.'

'Not at all,' said Zarl. 'You never get that idea among the best people. Love is like a silver kettle specially boiled for tea, most perfect if plucked from the flame before it goes too far. Leave it a moment too long and it fizzles over, putting out the flame and releasing the gas fumes. Either that or it just boils and boils till the water has gone and the kettle is destroyed.'

'Then,' stammered Cedd, 'Do you disbelieve in love, or only in marriage?'

'Marriage is the colossical example of carrying love too far.'

'But, it would be convenient to know how far you consider love should be carried?'

'To the point of perfection, like the silver kettle – that point where experience could not be added without tarnishing imagination.'

'Couldn't that be a little unsatisfactory?' murmured Cedd.

But Zarl said that compensation was invested in obviating satiety.

Of course Cedd did not propose in my presence. I extracted this under cross examination when he had departed.

'As for Frereton,' said Zarl, 'Shall I dismiss him now or leave him on the boil a little longer to cure Cedd of presumption?'

'Leave him on the boil. Through him we can get news of the Tattingwood case – if any, and be kept in chocs and flowers.'

In my publicity operations I saw that Zarl also had the benefit of Percy, she his rightful mistress. This had a reper-cussion in Loane Street, Knightsbridge, which put Mme

Mabelle's enterprises on their feet, and more. Zarl and I were able to bank funds, and to take a taxi on wet days when we had lost our umbrella (a chronic state). We were well-groomed, this also, by the aid of Percy, almost became permanent with us. And Zarl would exclaim, 'Now to travel from Yakutsk to Russkoye-Ustye, two thousand miles by reindeer! Those little darlings not any taller than one's waist, who paw up the moss from under the snow; and then to Bulun on the Lena. If this luck holds and I can inspire some scientist explorer to investigate the second metacarpels of the birds of flight, or the barbules on the wings of the barbels, or any other goose chase on the Plokhaya Rietchka Ozera it would be just what I need. There is the black brant, and the thick-beaked bean goose, and the large white-fronted goose, and the small snow goose, very rare. And the rare roseate gull, which nests at the Kolyma Delta.'

I kept out of the news in every shape and form. Only a bad publicity merchant fouls his own limelight. He must leave it clear for his subjects if he wants the press platoons on his side.

CHAPTER 21

Inspector Frereton was permitted to remain on the boil for the sake of news. When the blue diamond had safely reappeared we insisted that it was now clear that Yusuf had not been able to steal it. His actions had been motivated by the idea that Percy really had taken it, a sound theory rooted in knowledge of monkeys. During an evening when Zarl was particularly winning, and served champagne for supper, Inspector Frereton admitted that Headquarters had nothing serious against the young Indian, and that no steps would be taken against him if he would appear and explain satisfactorily his actions during the early hours of that December Sunday morning. The Inspector confessed that there never had been any clues to connect Yusuf with the murder – the only suspicion against him had been in connection with the gem. We were naturally eager to hear more but the Inspector was not so much on the boil, nor the champagne so potent, that he divulged professional secrets.

'You are no true vamp,' I said to Zarl, but Zarl said it was merely that she did not waste big shot on insignificant game.

Between us we had contacts with Indians of many grades. We enjoyed some of them as interesting and affectionate friends, and so spread word among them. This resulted in Yusuf's reappearance. He was a student of high standing, whose family was making tremendous sacrifices so that he might pursue his studies in London.

It transpired that the blue diamond was actually one of the State jewels of a live reigning prince whose name, as a dictate of Imperial good form, had been carefully suppressed. Lord

Tattingwood's nickname for him had now varying musical comedy versions ranging from Bong to Bopp-whoop. This gentleman had given the diamond to Ydonea in Paris, but the chauffeur guardian appointed by the father Rajah was merely an imaginative publicity agent's creation. In England various students occasionally earned something towards their education by this means.

Yusuf was an exemplary student in psychology, but reverses had made it difficult for him to carry on. He had entered the room where Zarl and I were sleeping at Tattingwood with the intention of taking Percy. He confessed that his temptation had had two legs, one to secure and secrete the Bongwallop gem and thereby reap a reward, the other to return the diamond to its proper place in India where the awakening masses were resentful that their Prince, the representative of Allah, should squander the State Jewels and make a spectacle of himself in a continental capital by supporting actresses, and in England by owning racehorses.

This would have been a graceful act of brotherhood towards a countryman of different faith. Yusuf was a Hindu. He earnestly assured us that Percy Macacus Rhesus y Osterley would have been quite safe with him. He was a vegetarian, against the shedding of the blood of any animal, and would not have hurt a hair of the monkey's coat. Percy was, he insisted, an Indian temple monkey, and as he came from Africa, her forebears probably had been taken there by Indian indentured labour. Yusuf was revolted by people who made friends of animals, and at the same time would either eat them or torture and chase them, and call it sport. His name, which was Gulam, indicated a flower. To call him Yusuf was analagous to indifference regarding the political and religious chasms existing between Catholic Sinn Feiners and Ulstermen of the Loyal Lodge of Orangemen.

Gulam Das, or Yusuf, as he had better remain for convenience for the duration of this history, had felt the effects of my blow for some time. It had caught him on the left side of the face and given him a terrific black eye, but we forgave each other for our reciprocal suspicions and started an interesting acquaintanceship on fellow feeling about them.

He had secreted himself in Lady Tattingwood's apartments

upon returning from Supersnoring and disguised himself in the purple bed quilt as soon as Lady Tattingwood went out. How he returned to London and was hidden in the Indian colony was of interest to the police, and they were able to check his statements. His professors had been informed that he had had to depart for India suddenly to see his dying mother, and could do nothing but accept the statement.

I had no charge to bring against Yusuf but that of his failure to use his handkerchief in the Reading Room of the British Museum, and I suggested a regulation requiring the use of handkerchiefs to place beside that other against licking the fingers, and the need for enforcing both, but the C.I.D. said that that was for the Director of the British Museum.

I regretted having whacked and suspected Yusuf, and now acknowledged that he was a handsome and engaging youth. I made amends by asking Ydonea to give him some part of the reward which she had offered, but which neither Zarl nor I could accept. Ydonea made it the occasion for a fresh burst of publicity and flew back from the Riviera for the purpose. Yusuf was forgiven his suspicious antics, his more suspicious disappearance, and reinstated in that society which he adorns in Bloomsbury. The friends who had sheltered him were likewise forgiven their distrust of law in a foreign country; and also, a certain Maharajah, in London for some round table conference, or conference around some table or another, was able to say a word in the right quarter to put things straight.

But the murderer was still unapprehended. The clearing of Yusuf and me in respect of the disappearance of the diamond and the alibi exonerating the absent airman, left the mystery of who had killed Stopworth more than ever a mystery.

Shortly after the reappearance of the blue diamond, Ydonea received a letter from Jimmy Wengham from some place in Africa, where he had had a forced landing and where the letter had awaited a mailman for weeks. In it was enclosed a pawnbroker's ticket from Paris for the yellow diamond. This had been his means of raising funds for the flight. This is what he meant by taking Ydonea's monetary help as well as her plane, and the diamond was safe. She had only to present the ticket and pay the few hundred pounds which he had raised. Jimmy meant to fly to Cape Town for a start and then do some cross world flight.

Nothing more of him or the Puss Moth had been heard. There had been rumours of planes in various places but they could never be run to earth. It seemed as if Jimmy had crashed in some wild place. Ydonea had another flood of publicity out of this. Jimmy, she stated, was sure to be in some new place, he might have lost the plane but would turn up in due time with incredible adventures to his score.

Yusuf's reappearance and statement raised a new point in the evidence. Upon their own insistence, two people had been cracked by my broom on that December night, and I had not admitted hitting more than one. Inspector Frereton had to revise the position in face of this, and asked me to appear at Scotland Yard. He did me the honour to consult rather than heckle me; thanks to Zarl's protection, also to the entries in the dead Chief Inspector's diary commending my acumen in observation and deduction; and because every statement I had made was verified by events.

I was asked if I had struck twice with the broom on the fatal night. I said no, emphatically no. Then I was asked to say which story I considered true. I promptly said Yusuf's. I placed furniture in relation to doors and bed to illustrate the improbability of breaking an elbow unless it had been raised.

'Then am I to understand Miss Carrington, that you have known all along that you were not responsible for Lady Tattingwood's injury?'

'I only *thought*, I couldn't *know*. I allowed for the possibility of falling asleep, as everyone suggested, which could have made me woozy about my actions.'

'But why did you not point out these possibilities?'

'You must remember, Inspector, that when you are seeking information, you rely upon cross questioning, and repress any tendency to loquacity. You must also remember that no credence was given to my statement of how the dagger came into my room. My statement had no corroboration by anyone but hysterical Mammy Lou; and you suggested that the form she saw was Lady Tattingwood fleeing to her husband's room. You must remember that the dagger was flung malevo¹-ently just where I should have stopped it had I left the stretcher where it was placed by the housemaid. It seemed that there was someone at large who had no scruples so long as he got the gem, and I did not want to make statements that would further endanger my safety. I had to *think* my way out of it. It seemed to me during the cross-questioning that the aim was to prove me a daughter of joy or a thief rather than to find the murderer.'

'A mere matter of procedure.'

'I accept your apology, but you must remember that this was my first experience of such procedure, and it disinclined me to be expansive.'

'Did you know of anyone who would have been willing to kill you for the gem, or for any other reason?'

'I never suspected there was such a person in the world, till we found that dreadful dagger. Was there anyone with a motive for killing the Chief Inspector?'

'Not that we know of, but a man in his position runs the risk of dangerous enemies. Someone besides you may have seen him take the yellow diamond from Miss Zaltuffrie and not have known that it had been taken from him in turn by Wengham.'

'Have you any clues?'

'None strong enough to warrant an arrest. Have you?'

'I have no means of obtaining clues; I can only think.'

Inspector Frereton is well-suited to his work. He has a disciplined temper and is willing to learn. Also, to render him human and friendly, was his infatuation for Zarl, near whom I stood. 'I wish you would tell me what you think about Lady Tattingwood's injury,' he said.

'She probably met the apparition that threw the dagger, and in a struggle to silence her, he judoed her arm, and it really was all that she could do to reach her husband's room.'

'The weakness of that theory is, why didn't she say so? Why should she take advantage of your story with the broom, which she must have heard from her husband before the doctor discovered her injury? She was supposed to be desperately ill as well as injured, but she wasn't too ill to mug up a story.'

'Quite. But you must regard the evidence about her attachment to the Chief Inspector. I believe that she went to his room, and encountered the murderer just after the act. That was the terrible shock, and it was merely to save her reputation that the poor lady made up the story of being hit by me.'

'So you considered that too.'

'Rather!' I did not confess that I had seen Clarice actually enter Stopworth's room, and fancied that I heard a cry. I had not quite made up my own mind as to whether she met the murderer there or elsewhere. She had met some brute somewhere, to account for her broken elbow. It was possible that she might have tripped and fallen in her flight, but not likely.

'If the murderer was after the yellow diamond, he did not search for it, as nothing at all was disturbed, and it does not look as if he was interrupted, or he wouldn't have had time to open your door and throw the dagger in there; and he did that after the murder, as the blood on the weapon proved.'

'Well, my door was opened with a key very softly and easily and it was a Yale lock.'

'An expert can open those locks with a hair-pin. A non-expert must have had a key.'

'Who?'

'It would be helpful to know.'

'There is the theory that Captain Stopworth must have opened his door to some voice he knew?'

'Or one he *thought* he knew – some people are wonderful mimics.'

'And that would be someone in the house, or one of his own assistants.'

'It is the difficulty of establishing a feasible motive.'

'Someone who had been gambling and was in low water.'

'Everyone gambles these days. There was a wide choice of people strapped for funds, nearly everyone from that Elephant Hunter to Wengham; and nearly *all* the ladies. The Elephant Hunter was a tremendous mimic.'

'I never heard him say a word.'

'During the war he used to entertain the soldiers at Tatting-wood by mimicking all the officers and stage stars . . . It may of course have been someone determined to 'get' the Chief Inspector for a long time. One of Miss Zaltuffrie's private

squad may have been got at to allow a substitute to imper-
sonate him.'

'But such a person would not have flung a dagger at me?
It could scarcely be considered a practical joke.'

'Some people have an advanced sense of humour. Did
anyone special know the position of your stretcher?'

'Nearly everyone, I should think, because Percy was such
a puppet show that no one was above calling upon him from
the butler to the kitchen maid.'

'We can't get any fresh clue unless through Lady
Tattingwood.'

'I haven't heard how she is lately. Miss Osterley has not
been allowed to see her yet, but that cannot go on indefinitely.
She must get better or pass out altogether.'

'She has passed out – *mentally*. She is in a home for such
cases,' said Inspector Frereton. 'That is why we cannot get
the rights of her story, and the solution hangs on it.'

CHAPTER 22

We knew that Lady Tattingwood was seriously ill. Zarl kept in telephone touch regularly, but the answer was always the same, that Lady Tattingwood was going on as well as could be expected, but was not yet permitted any visitors except the immediate members of her family. Lord Tattingwood had given Zarl to understand that his wife's life had lain in the balance for weeks. She was surrounded by specialists of one sort or another headed by Sir Philmore Galstone.

My news from Inspector Frereton shocked Zarl. 'Oh, surely it can't be true,' she exclaimed. 'But poor old Clarice was never a strong character. People could sway her. That was what made her so lovable and kind, and I suppose the shock was too much for her in every way. I must get hold of Swithwulf personally.'

She wrote him a kind letter without divulging what she had heard, and suggesting that they should lunch together. She apologised for carelessness on the grounds that her business never allowed her a moment for her friends.

Later she was depressed by her luncheon with Swithwulf. The report of Clarice's mental condition was unfortunately true. He had done his best to keep it quiet, hoping that she would recover in time, when her arm mended and if she could surmount the heart trouble, but she now needed special care. He did not advise her friends to see her, as she did not know anyone. Lord Tattingwood himself visited her regularly. He had lived beside her while she was in the nursing home, which had fitted-in, as he was suffering a good deal himself with some indeterminable gastric trouble.

Zarl reported that he looked saggy and yellow, very thin and dispirited. 'Poor old Swithy, I liked him better than I ever did before. He seemed really anxious about Clarice. He has found out that he cares for her as well as her money. Perhaps friendship can grow in marriage if there has been no love to spoil.'

'Will Lady Tattingwood recover, or is it one of those hopeless cases?'

'The doctors think it depends on her being safe from any further shock. They can't risk the excitement of the most ordinary visitors, it appears, but Swithwulf says the doctors are of no more use than a pack of hounds when it comes to a wind-up.'

Any light that Lady Tattingwood could have thrown on the mystery of Stopworth's death was thus indefinitely postponed.

It was pigeonholed as an unsolved case. Inspector Frereton said it had become anybody's case, in a manner of speaking. Unless Lady Tattingwood recovered sufficiently to make some fresh deposition, it might remain unsolved for ever. A confession might come from some unconnected source or never come at all, but when Inspector Frereton called on us, I could detect that his mind was still on the case. To bring the murderer to justice would be a triumph for him. His mind worked around the disappearance of the sheet with which the Elephant Hunter and Wengham had amused themselves after Percy and I left the dining hall, and the fact that particles of linen had been found in the ashes brought from the fireplaces. This strengthened the theory that it could have been no outsider who threw the dagger. There might have been a gangster crack among Ydonea's people, or among the Tattingwood household. Or, the linen thread might not have been a piece of the sheet, which could have been disposed of outside the house. The reward offered to anyone who could throw any light on the matter remained unclaimed.

The public forgot the tragedy. Many another succeeded it on the torrent of modern life. Winter passed and summer came again, with Percy frolicking rapturously in any sunshine to be found. I took him to Hyde Park for exercise. This ordeal taught me to sympathise with the King and Queen, and the

Prince of Wales, for the crowds that a monkey can unfailingly collect would fill any cinema daily. Wherever Percy disported himself all grades of headgear from top hats through peewits down to caps, all accents from hee-haw to what-abhat it, all ages from twins in prams to persons in wheel chairs, all minds from nit-wits and morons to professors of high sensibility, and business successes, seemed equally to enjoy the gambols and graces of our little friend. This showed us that Ydonea understood the mob on some points. 'When she comes back I'll see that she gets a film about Percy. That peanut Cedd must make a continuity, Percy will do the rest.'

Ydonea was fulfilling a contract, some scenes of which were being shot in Alaska, and Cedd's ambition in her direction was at present in abeyance.

The social season went its way with its usual froth. Lord Tattingwood asked Zarl to luncheon with him at the Berkeley and to go down to Tattingwood for a week-end. Percy remained with me.

Zarl reported one of the saddest week-ends she had shared.

Lord Tattingwood was thinner and yellower than when she last saw him, leant heavily on a big stick and would starve but for Benger's food, which he ungratefully anathematised as 'blasted slops.' The party was a queer collection, presided over, and, apparently mustered, by Miss Bitcalf-Spillbeans, the inconsequent connection who had been there at the time of the tragedy. She asked Zarl if the odious little monkey was still alive and as troublesome and spiteful as ever, and Zarl said that Percy's spite was a matter of reflection.

Lord Tattingwood had seemed to cling to Zarl. The house had a musty, unlived-in air, but the grounds were Lord Tattingwood's idol, and lovelier than Zarl had ever seen them. He showed them to her from every angle, pointing out fresh vistas. 'A man might sell his soul for that,' he remarked.

And Zarl responded 'I wonder if he would think it worth it in the end.'

'Nothing is worth anything in the end, except physical comfort, but in the beginning a man wouldn't be a man if he did not take what he wanted when he could,' her host had said, and turned the talk to Lady Tattingwood.

He spoke of her with evident feeling and hoped everything

would be all right for her in the end. He complained of his loneliness, and asked Zarl to come and stay as often as she could, and to bring any of her friends. He even asked to be remembered to me.

The doctors were no good, he complained. They were advising the knife for him, but he was against that. 'I could give a limb with comparative equanimity, but don't want any of those cows of surgeons groping about among my vitals for their own entertainment.'

Cow in the profane Australian rendering was an expletive he had picked up from Zarl. She asked him if he could account for Clarice's mental collapse, and his theory, told in confidence, coincided with mine.

He believed she had been with Stopworth when the murderer appeared, had herself been assailed, but escaped, and would say nothing of the matter because it would disclose her relations with Stopworth. 'Though Gawd knows I should not have cut up about it – knew all the time for matter of that – but people who live in glass houses should not throw stones – eh?'

Everyone was sorry for Lord Tattingwood, ill and lonely, consoling himself with the beauty of his grounds while the spirit of emptiness stalked the noble pile, now open to tourists two days a week upon payment of two shillings per head.

A summer of splendid leafage and intermittent sunshine ran its course. I had lost track of Yusuf. Nothing more was heard of Jimmy Wengham. No wreckage of a machine which could have been his had yet been found. His aged father had almost given him up for lost. Lord Tattingwood reposted a letter from 'That wall-eyed Elephant Hunter somewhere in equatorial Africa,' who stated that one of his boys had described a man who had fallen from the sky into a savage tribe and was being detained as a god or devil or something. The Elephant Hunter suggested an expedition to investigate the rumour but needed funds for bearers and ammunition.

'It might be just a ruse on his part,' was Lord Tatting-wood's comment,' to get funds for one of his pic-nics. A queer fellow that. A lot more in him than ever comes out, if you ask me.'

Upon this Zarl remarked that she hoped so or he would be as hollow as a tom-tom.

The various incidents of life come together in a series of climaxes like bouquets. Then the flowers wither and the bouquets drop apart. We had gathered at Tattingwood that Saturday afternoon in December in a colourful bouquet, and now the sole remaining stalk was the Baron himself, ill and suffering, but making regular visits to poor lost Clarice.

CHAPTER 23

Autumn was with us. The way to the British Museum was sodden with the last of the plane leaves. Permanent twilight seemed to have settled on us. We plodded along. Zarl was overcome with wanderlust.

'Here we sit like the outdated models at Mme Tussaud's,' she would exclaim, 'prematurely in the dim twilight of our lives, and we ought to be starting now on that thousand mile trek by reindeer from Verkoyansk back to Bulun to see the ice break on the Lena.'

'You must hang some tastier carrots before the nose of some ornithologist.'

'I do, but they all want to go to the easy places, and it is Siberia that drives me wild with longing. Nearly a year since I made up my mind, and what have I got – not even an expedition to Margate in a backless bathing suit. No experiments beyond Cedd and Frereton and a few unmentionable oddments. We could have solved the murder mystery if we had put our minds to it. Even that would have been better than nothing. Something has got to happen.'

Then she had a letter from Lord Tattingwood asking her to call on him in the Nursing Home to which his wife had been brought nearly a year since. Suffering, as do many men of his years, but refusing an operation, he had gone through hell during the last six months, and came to the knife too late.

Zarl was shocked. She reported that she could see Death in the room when she entered. 'I forgot to write to the poor old thing lately. I wish I had rung up or something, but one never has time.'

Lord Tattingwood had specially requested to see me. There could be no mistake, 'The young woman got up as a Dago maid in charge of that damn' little monkey, the week-end of the murder. Tell her to come soon, or it will be too late. I have to play out my hand with her.'

I was surprised by the request to see me — the fancy of a sick man probably, but later, Zarl was informed by Lord Tattingwood's physician that he held to it.

After that, he was removed to Tattingwood upon his own demand, and the eminent physician who attended him, took me down with him one foggy December morning, just a year from my other visit to the lovely place.

Everything was arranged in the graciously hospitable manner of the English country house where the entertaining of guests is an ancient tradition. The physician went directly to his patient. I was taken to the library where a splendid fire was just ripe, and offered wine, which I refused. Miss Bitcalf-Spillbeans was not in evidence. It was the same butler, and we chatted about things, including the tragic week-end.

'Things have never been right here since then,' the old man said sadly.

When Sir Philmore descended we had luncheon together. He informed me that there was little now to be done for his patient but administer opiates. He was dozing and would send for me immediately after luncheon. 'You will probably have to stay all night,' Sir Philmore remarked. 'It is kind of you to humour a dying man who has suffered shockingly and borne it stoically. I greatly admire Lord Tattingwood's fortitude.'

My expression probably changed when Sir Philmore spoke of a dying man. 'You must be prepared for a sad change in Lord Tattingwood's appearance. Don't be too shocked. Release cannot be far away now. And do not be distressed by his hallucinations. Humour him.'

It was nearly three o'clock when a messenger came for me, and a nursing sister, in the uniform of the London Hospital, ushered me into the sick room.

Despite the physician's warning I was unspeakably shocked

by the spectacle before me. Lord Tattingwood had been felled by cancer, that scourge so dreaded that we seek to evade its very name. He was freshly shaven and exquisitely tended. All that skill, money and high position commanded were his.

He did not offer his great hand. It lay outside the covers. The thick red hair on skin contracted by emaciation, made it startlingly ape-like. It was almost as hairy but not nearly so exquisitely fashioned as Percy's fairy hand. The skin, yellow and deathlike, was tightly drawn over the bones of the head. Only the small, cunning eyes ruthlessly held their purpose and showed that reason was still fully enthroned despite the merciful opiates, the only aid that civilisation can yet give the victim in this grim battle.

'Well, young woman! It looks as if you had won, but I may have a trump for the last trick,' was his greeting.

I did not know how to reply so waited for him to continue. He asked me to recall the nurse, and he ordered her to give him another needle, as the dose had been insufficient.

'Don't go!' he said to me. 'You'll find the view from the end window rather fine.'

The view was more than fine. It was a traditional, ancestral, historical English view. One has to see these views and have the feeling for them thoroughly to understand. 'It must be wonderful to have that for one's own, for that to be home,' I said, returning to the bedside.

'It has been. But what about the price?'

'Do you regret the price?'

'What do you know of the price of such things?' he asked with a keen look.

'Nothing whatever. It was a random remark to make conversation.'

'That's strange. Your first remark too, fitted in. It was to tell you about the price that I brought you here.'

I waited for him to continue.

'Go and lock that door,' he ordered, pointing to the one through which the nurse had disappeared. I did not like doing this, but I was there to humour a man near death. He then asked me to see that other doors were locked, and to look behind curtains and pieces of furniture. At length he was satisfied.

'I don't want anyone to hamstring my last play,' he remarked. 'Come now and sit so I shan't have to shout.'

I sat as he prescribed, taking care not to move those tragic tubes protruding from the bedclothes into vessels, revolted by the cruel fungi which prey on all things living. Eventually I was placed to his satisfaction.

'Did you find out who killed Stopworth?' he asked.

'No.'

'Not as clever as you seem, perhaps . . . One of the unsolved murders. Life is full of them . . . What do you think of the police handling of it? Why couldn't they solve a striking case like that, when they have done such ripping things – eh?'

'Perhaps it was a sporadic outbreak on the part of the killer, and so left the police helpless.'

'What do you mean by that?' he demanded sharply. 'Out with it, tell me your reason for saying that?'

'Just a theory . . . I must not weary you.'

'It would entertain me, and you are here to do as I want – just exactly what I want this time. Tell me your theory.'

'Merely that I think the chief difference between the C.I.D. and common outsiders is that the C.I.D. are trained and experienced: they are expert at tracking down regular criminals, know whom to suspect and where to pounce. They can also follow a murderer if he has done a number of crimes because of similarity in method, or when there is a motive, and so on. But supposing somebody like me, or yourself, were to break out and kill someone for no apparent motive and just march off leaving no clue, there would be nothing to go on, and Capt. Stopworth's death seems to be a case in point.'

'You're too damn' clever by far. A woman who reasons things out and can't be bluffed is not natural – she deserves to come to Stopworth's end. Major force is the thing to apply to such hussies. Brains in women is a sign of decadence – look at the world to-day . . . that proves it.'

'Yes, I should say its parlous condition could be imputed to lack of ethical intelligence and womanly common sense.'

'There you go, sticking in some meaning that you think I can't get . . . I haven't time to waste on slim-jim clack . . . open the box on the table,' he concluded peremptorily.

It was a smallish case containing among other things, two ancient pistols elaborately ornamented in silver, and an up-to-date Webley Revolver. He asked for the revolver and, when I handed it, laid it on the bedclothes on his chest. 'See anything there you recognise?' he continued.

'You mean the dagger?'

'Yes. The police collared the other one; it's the fellow of the one I threw into your bedroom a year ago, the one you stuck into Stopworth.'

He must have seen a little of my shock, though I reacted against it as quickly as possible. I recalled Sir Philmore Galstone's murmur of hallucinations, and for the first time felt appreciative of that physician's eminence. 'I don't think I am tall enough to have done that,' I remarked with what indifference I could assume.

'Huh! They were all too stupid when reconstructing the crime to put that heavy footstool outside Stopworth's door – the one I gave you to weight that filthy little ape. On that you'd be more than tall enough. Piff! the blade went home like a bird, didn't it, as it did not strike a rib or anything. Then all you had to do was to take the footstool back next door and close the door on Stopworth. Juxtaposition was good for you – eh?'

'I see,' I said, humouring a madman, but almost voiceless. 'And what do you consider was the motive for the crime?'

'Money of course – the blue diamond. You knew he had the blue diamond all the time for safety. I know all about the stunt of recovering it later from the monkey. You must have pulled wires to get that through. No one would believe it would stay in the animal so long. Got too hot for your fingers, and you thought it was safer to step out from under, as the Americans say. . . .

'The Zaltuffrie's squeak about losing it was all for a publicity stunt. It was passed to the Inspector, and you knew that, the same as you knew about the yellowboy. It all seemed nice and easy – sporadic murder – he! he! Caught you nicely on your own theory there, didn't I?'

I thought with great uneasiness of the locked door; and the bell rope on the other side of the bed from me, close to his hand, and that revolver – evidently loaded. Those awful tubes – to excite him might bring his death there and then, or my own by his hand. There was no way of summoning his nurse. I calmed myself and bided my time, for some turn that would bring deliverance. In my consciousness arose tales of people humouring madmen till they could escape. Though alarmed I was not yet panic striken.

'When you threw that dagger into Miss Osterley's bedroom, did you know that I had shifted my bed?' I suddenly demanded.

'No.'

'Then you meant to kill me?'

'Why not?'

'Oh, simply that it is not usual, is it?'

'I didn't care whether I killed you or not. I should have enjoyed hearing you yelp.'

Lord Tattingwood's attack upon me was more unnerving because he appeared entirely sane. There seemed to be a twinkle of devilish humour in his small ugly eyes, and he was as free from any sign of delirium or excitement as I had ever seen anyone. I was fascinated by his apparent enjoyment of the situation.

He continued: 'The satisfaction of private killing is lost because it is not safe to tell about it . . . the fun of shooting big game is soon over if there is no smoking-room crowd to blow to about it . . . As for motive, the smallest motives do a chap for anything if the lust for it is on him . . . I'm going to tell you the story of my life.'

'I should like to hear it,' I said, seeing here a splendid opportunity of gaining time and perhaps wearying him so that he would fall asleep under the opiates, or that his attendant would come.

'You bet it's going to be interesting . . . I came here a gawky ugly devil of a lad . . . You didn't want me that night – had the impudence to trifle with me – and stuck a pin in me when I touched you. Stuck a pin in me in my own house! I'll stick this dagger in you before we've finished, if I feel like it.' He felt the point with his thumb. I suppressed a shudder.

'I was the son of a poor parson, second cousin of the fifteenth Baron. They were going to put me in the church! Ha! . . . My smug cousin-uncle, and his priggish heir! The

lovely Ecgwulf George St. Erconwald Spillbeans . . . The first
girl I cared about wouldn't look at me, because I was ugly,
and because Ecgwulf was to be the sixteenth Tattingwood.

'It made me long to murder him . . . He did not care for
this place at all . . . a puling fellow who wanted to get into
a laboratory and make stinks, and who despised soldiers
and footballers, and good shots, and steeplechase riders, and
everything I was . . . Pshaw! . . . Tattingwood, the only thing
I ever loved. I never had a mistress, excepting the Nigger
wenches in South Africa, who gave me the satisfaction that
I get by looking out that window into those woods . . . The
Boer War came . . . made big game hunting seem as tame as
firin' at a few monkeys . . . got some of the fire out of me
. . . They gave me a V.C. I earned it too, in the way V.C.'s
are earned . . . It taught me that human life is so trumpery
. . . a man is nothing more than a rabbit or deer when it
comes to that – whiff! and he's dead flesh!

'When I came back from South Africa, my fine cousin was
here, trembling at the thought of the responsibility that must
soon be his . . . an inside like those grubs they fish with in
Australia . . . It would take him from his science laboratory
. . . and I would have given three souls, if I had them, to
possess Tattingwood . . . Go and look out the other window
. . . do you see that wood?'

I went and looked out as directed, expecting a shot or
dagger in the back but hoping that his story might continue
until deliverance.

'Ecgwulf and I went out shooting one day and we separated
at the top there . . . look at those two big elms against the
sky . . . I got home before him. He was so long coming that
we had to go and look for him. The fool had shot himself
getting over the stile up there . . . Couldn't go after a rabbit
without making a mess of it, though he could find his way
among galipots and things that were much more dangerous
. . . Come and sit down again.'

I tried to improve my position, but he was insistent even
to an inch, and the big hairy hand was caressing the dirk.
When my position was to his satisfaction he leaned forward,
his glances seeking to pierce me with demoniac intensity, as

he said, 'I had extraordinary luck in that.' I nodded. He underlined the next phrase with the skill of a great actor.

'No *one ever suspected that it was not an accident* . . .'

The sparrows could be heard outside the window, the coals dropping in the grate inside. My tension tightened with the halt in his story.

'That was another unsolved murder at Tattingwood.'

The hallucinations engendered by pressure on the spinal nerve, and opiates, were responsible for this, I tried to think, but the grim satisfaction of Lord Tattingwood, his calm clarity assured me that he was speaking the bald truth. If insane, it was not in the form of loss of his faculties. He was dreadfully fiendishly true, I felt in my inmost places. The sense of unreality clung rather to me. I was seemingly entrapped in a nightmare, thrust from actuality into phantasmagoria. I said nothing – petrified – but a comfortable petrification now. The awful terror which had sickened me had miraculously left me. There lay the dying man confessing crimes, imaginary or real. Soon he would be among the countless hosts of the dead, and I perhaps with him. Others had faced similar situations. They had gone without recording their emotions. I had often admired the pluck of people in like position, thinking that I should have become hysterical under the strain, but apparently there was only one way to act.

Lord Tattingwood continued, terrible and cruel. 'I came into the place while I was still popular because of the Boer war. The girl did not have any trouble in turning her affections to me now . . . but I always despised her for it . . . Clarice's was a better deal . . . No one ever suspected. It made it dull, but civilians are a mouldy pack of rabbits. How can they be anything else, and growing softer every year . . . I've often had the temptation to stick a knife into a few of them just to see if they are as frail as I remembered them. Sometimes when the lust was on me, I had a rough time holding in. It took me that night when you came in with the ape and we were pitching the dagger. It seemed to me funny. I'm not a wasteful man, and I looked around to pick someone that would mean killing two birds with the one stone.

'There was that Stopworth beauty. Had Clarice nearly weaned away from me . . . and that would have been the end of Tattingwood. There was no need to kill Stopworth for that though . . . I could have spiked his guns easily, but I took the easiest way to save a lot of fuss and feathers and to ease the lust that was on me. I had you as a second string. You were making fun of me – meant to doublecross me, as that Yankee moving doll would have said. I hate clever women . . . that's why I have used little drabs. One housemaid it worth half a dozen of the high steppers, and you, a foreigner, a flunkey, had the audacity to stick a pin in me at my own entertainment!'

He looked for a moment as if he were going to faint. Having lost my fear, I begged him to desist, but he said, 'No, I must tell you the whole thing. It was as easy as eating gooseberry pie, wasn't it?' He chuckled as if in pleasant recollection. 'I expect all the unsolved murders would be equally simple if the killers confessed . . . I just put on some gloves and a sheet, that one down in the dining room. I saw it as I went that way to get the dagger out of the lounge. In case anyone should be prowling about, I cut a couple of holes for my eyes, and set off. I couldn't find the dagger we had been using, so I took its mate. I turned off the lights in the gallery as I passed. Not a soul did I see but that blasted old black woman, and I flapped my arms and breathed loudly and put the fear of the Devil into her . . . never saw anything so funny. She must be trembling and yelping still . . . But that was on the return journey.

'I saw the light in Stopworth's window from the terrace. I knocked softly on his door and spoke in a low voice. There was no reply. I scraped on the door, but still no reply. I had a key. That suite was my own once and I have always kept the key that was supposed to be lost. I'm a 'tec in my own way, though I may not have looked it . . . There was the bobby stretched out dead as a fish, and my dirk sticking through him . . . You had been the little early bird, and got there before me . . . I was so mad, I could have dragged you out of bed and spitted you, not for killing him but for getting ahead of me – doublecrossing me . . .'

Fear invaded me again. This was an unexpected turn to the Stopworth murder, and these were suspicions, not hallucinations. Others too could harbour them. Inspector Frereton – his apparent bewitchment by Zarl, evidently a sleuth's tactics.

'This comes as a complete, a horrible surprise, Lord Tattingwood,' I managed to murmur. 'What did you do?'

'I pulled my dagger out of Stopworth. There was not a sound anywhere. I opened your door – no sound but breathing – Miss Osterley's I suppose. I just tossed in the dagger to put a frill on the affair. I hoped to hear you squeak, but there was no sound, so I skedaddled back to base.'

'Did you tell this to the police?'

'You'd like to know that, wouldn't you? But you must listen to my whole story . . . My weak point was the sheet. It was dabbled in blood – must have trodden in it when I was getting the dagger out. That would have been incriminating, and what a triumph for you, to have me taken in the act. If I had had my buttons done up I should have flung it somewhere out in the grounds or into your room at the first go. But owing to that squawking old Negress I could not risk a second trip. I decided to burn it. I made up my fire and meant to burn the thing in sections . . . I put the clean dagger back in its place and was just starting on the sheet when Clarice came knocking on my door and crying out. I guessed that she had been to Stopworth's room, and would wake the house if I did not take hold of things firmly. I could have let her rip only for that sheet. She said she had a pain and had come for brandy, but I could see that she was nearly demented with fright. She never had any stamina.

'There was nothing for it but to quieten her and get the sheet out of sight in a bundle, and risk throwing it out of a window at the other end of the house into the shrubbery. At first I think she really meant to pretend, to hide her fright, and that she had been to Stopworth's room, for fear of how I'd act, but she was too elaborately got-up in a negligee fit for the film doll, to be honestly paying me a visit to get brandy for a stomach ache. I tried to keep her in the dressing-room but she shivered and asked if I had a fire. Then she saw I had just made up the fire and was in dressing-gown and slippers.

'She still talked about the colic, but my being up – with a fire at that hour was unusual, and turning round, she caught sight of the sheet all over blood. She looked at me and would have shrieked aloud if I hadn't taken strong measures. She went off her head ... I had to silence her ... I may have been over rough ... but I silenced her. Shock and pain together broke her spirit. I threatened her ... my threats don't matter now ... They were effective. She moaned that I had killed him, but I said I had not, that I had gone to his room to do so, but someone had been before me. I pretended that that was herself, and the poor devil collapsed altogether. She always allowed herself to be dominated. I took the high hand. Said I knew all about her goings on with Stopworth, and could bear no more. If she said one word I threatened to say that I had found her in Stopworth's arms and had taken the short way for wronged husbands. I also threatened her that her precious youngster would not be safe.'

'Poor thing!

'Poor old Clarice, a tight corner, but you're in a worse one now, so keep your mawkishness for yourself. She really believed I killed Stopworth so I worked on that. I was a bit hard on her ... She was never a beauty, but she was harmless and knew how to let a man alone ... She was thoroughly broken and desperately ill – neurasthenic – and a husband has a great pull, in spite of the suffragettes. She was helpless against me. She has no chance in face of my solicitude, and is held by fears for her daughter.'

'Is that what unhinged her mind?'

'Her mind is not unhinged. Her turn is coming now. Old Philmore was a ripping scout for this, a great expert ha! ha! but he never guessed how clever I was. A great expert is easily manipulated ... But Clarice's turn is coming now. My game is up. I have come to the last trench, the last kopje, the last round of shot, and Tattingwood Hall is no good to me now ... As for my sons – Cedd is not so bad – but I never cared for either of them. I despised their mother for caring more for Tattingwood than the man; though I should not have blamed her for that ... inconsistent to blame others for being like myself ... The only son I cared for I could never acknowledge, and he was killed in the war.'

I saw with dismay that he was not wearying – was sustained diabolically, was enjoying himself.

'My little joke is almost ended. You see I am not such a milksop as you thought me when you stuck a pin in me after the racket about my tiepin.'

His hand again caressed the revolver. 'Bring me the packet in that drawer – of the escritoire – the right one, top. Yes, that's it,' he said as I held up a small sealed packet about the size of a fountain pen in case. 'Now, that big envelope.'

It was of linen such as used for briefs. 'And there is a small sealed envelope too ... Yes, that's the one.'

When the things were before him, he bound the sharp point of the dagger in a handkerchief and placed it with the smaller packet and sealed envelope in the big one. He looked at me and laughed, and I looked for delirium in those small cunning eyes, but surely it was nothing but amusement that gleamed there, devilish enjoyment of the situation in which he had placed me. He had confessed to going to Stopworth's room with the intention of killing him, why should he act to me as if avenging Stopworth's death?

'You haven't yelped or turned green around the gills yet,' he said with a ghastly grin. 'You think I'm delirious and that you can handle me and escape, or that I'll fall asleep, or that you can grab the pistol or dagger, but one move my lady, and I shoot to kill, and I'll explain how I had you. In here,' – he indicated the sealed envelope – 'is a clear story of my doings in Stopworth's room that night. Everything that I told you except the facts of the other unsolved murder. I tell how I was forestalled by you, and your probable motive. Now, all that you have to do is fill in the blanks and I put it all in this envelope to be sealed up till I'm dead ...

'Now, come on, you can't say I'm not a good sportsman. While I am dying you have time to get away – Zarl will go with you to the Pole of Cold among the mosquitoes – you can have a run for your money. Take your choice of writing your confession and going, or being shot here and now ... Well, which is it?'

I looked steadily at him, down that fearful barrel. I am no heroine with nerves of steel to make brave gestures. My courage depends upon non-acceptance of situations as presented, but this one was so cogently presented that it made me sick and empty internally.

'I'll give you only five minutes more to decide,' he said, looking at the clock on the great mantel. Some of the lights had been on when I entered. He now turned a lot more on above the bed by means of a switch on a cord near to his hand.

'I cannot confess to what I did not do.'

'Pooh, you disappoint me ... showing the yellow streak. I'd have been easier on you had you owned up and told me how you did it. I'd enjoy that – and I always pay well for entertainment ... remember the tiepin.'

'See here,' I said. 'You say you are near your end, why spend your last hours in persecuting me? I was not in Stopworth's room that night, I swear. Also I do not know who was.'

I deliberately omitted Lady Tattingwood's name.

'If you killed Stopworth yourself, confess or not as you decide, but why go to your Maker ...'

'Shut up! I thought you would be above such slush. If you had seen as many men as I have curl up before their Maker – Bah! but here, the time is up.' He held the barrel towards me.

'I'll write,' I said. He grinned like a fiend.

He allowed me to bring pen and paper. I gained a few minutes by spoiling sheets, exaggerating the shaking of my hand, which was genuinely bad enough. 'What am I to write?' I said helplessly.

'Don't you try to doublecross me again. I have my specs. here and shall scrutinise every word with my finger on the trigger.'

If he was genuinely mad, I could calm him by writing a supposed confession, but it was not as simple as that. He seemed sane enough for mischievous purposes, and the Tattingwood murder was still unsolved. Who had killed Stopworth? That confession, bogus or otherwise, would do me no good. With it in existence in my writing, who was there to stand by me and say I had not done it? Zarl perhaps – but even she might be uncertain. She had been soundly asleep that night till I wakened her with the broom. And my experience of life had taught me that even the supposedly ethical will 'rat' without compunction if it saves any inconvenience to themselves.

No, I would not put a noose around my neck that way. I pretended to write. I wrote on steadily, illegible stuff about nothing. Lord Tattingwood grew restless. 'You have enough there to cover ten murders. Drop it, you are only stalling me.'

'Just one moment more.' I said, gathering my will and thinking I had rather be shot than hanged, or muddied by suspicion till life was insupportable. I suddenly rose with one of the jungle roars that I had cultivated to discipline Percy, scattering the revolver and dirk beyond his reach and rushed to unlock the door.

Lord Tattingwood pulled the bell cord. The nurse must have been anxious or curious. I almost collided with her.

'Is there a change?' she gasped. 'I thought I heard something.'

'Your patient is delirious,' I whispered 'and is overdoing his strength.'

The male attendant was immediately at hand. It was evident that Lord Tattingwood was now in great pain. I withdrew with the intention of escaping, but he called out that he wanted to see me again, and his valet came to conduct me to another room, but I sought the aid of the butler in telephoning Sir Philmore Galstone.

I told him, guardedly, that Lord Tattingwood had told me something so serious that I wanted him to know at once – that I needed his advice. Sir Philmore said that he was speaking at a meeting of the Medical Association that evening and could not see me till a late hour. I said I was returning to London and would see him no matter how late the hour.

I then asked for the physician in attendance and was told that the little friend at Supersnoring called every hour, and had missed one call because of his patient being so quietly occupied with me. He was due again now and when he came went straight to the patient. I insisted upon seeing him and the butler undertook to tell him. The doctor asked for me. His patient, he said, insisted upon seeing me again.

'Don't excite him, his condition is very grave.'

I refused to enter the room again unless the doctor and nurse accompanied me. 'He insisted upon me locking the door and then made the strangest accusations,' I ventured. 'Do you know that he even threatened to shoot me.'

'Oh, did he. He must have been over-excited. It does him no good to speak of old war days, and I'm sorry that you weren't told that his weapons have been rendered harmless. We took that precaution some time since.'

'Yes, but with regard to the solution of the tragedy here . . .'

'Oh, yes, did not Sir Philmore warn you of hallucinations. I say, and Sir Philmore agrees, that in a condition such as Lord Tattingwood's, the figments of . . .'

'But you must come with me, and don't leave me an instant alone with him.'

The doctor then entered with me.

Even a lay person could note the change in the patient in the half hour that had elapsed since my escape. Death was waiting in that splendid chamber and would not go away empty-handed. To me, throughout, his mind seemed clear, in spite of opiates, but I can only pit my belief against the testimony and attitude of experts. Was it possible that Lord Tattingwood's actions and words were entirely the result of opiates? Hardly.

'It was most obliging of you to come,' he said courteously. 'Well, my strength failed, but there is plenty here to prove my story to the hilt.' He indicated the long envelope, still on the bed. 'I shall leave this in trust to be opened at my death. Are you listening?'

'Yes. And will you not tell the doctor what you told me before he came?'

'Think I am wandering, don't you? I deny having said anything to you . . . you remember the tiepin, don't you?'

The half-laugh was ghastly on the mummified face. 'In here, duly signed and witnessed, is plenty to prove everything, and to clear everything up, and that Inspector fellow from Scotland Yard won't boggle at believing my story. He's been ready to pounce all the time like a harpy. And here, give this to little red-headed Zarl – with my love. Little Zarl, worth 'em all put together, in a scrum – heaps of wits of a womanly kind – none of this brainy stuff . . . Poor old Clarice, but she'll be all right when I am gone.'

'Well, good-bye Lord Tattingwood, may you find mercy and freedom from pain where everything is unravelled or forgotten.'

'What are you going to do about it?' he asked, with an ironic glint in the small burning eyes.

'I don't know. *Au revoir.*'

The doctor stayed with him. The nursing sister escorted me from the room. Outside the door I made another effort.

'Lord Tattingwood is very ill. He made the most extraordinary statements about the murder here a year ago.'

'Oh, yes, poor gentleman. His mind has gone round and round on that. Sir Philmore does not allow the subject to be mentioned . . . He is very low now. I don't know how he has lasted so long. It is easier when they have not such a constitution and such an iron will. He has been a brave patient – a great soldier – a V.C. He ought to have another V.C. where he is going for what he has been through.'

'It is terrible,' I murmured.

'I am so sorry he upset you, Miss Carrington.' It was evident that she did not know if I were an important friend, and was feeling her way. 'I forgot to warn you not to let him talk about those weapons and to tell you not to be frightened of them.'

'It is a pity that he is so alone.'

'He will not have anyone with him, but the heir is at hand all the time, and the other son, Mr. Cedd, is on the way home. His disease gives his Lordship notions.'

I tucked the letter that had been given me for Zarl in my handbag and went down the splendid staircase, up and down which I had chased Percy, and found the butler waiting to show me out. I stood a minute or two in the big hall where I had stood a year since with Percy in my arms, when all was gay and adventurous as a scene from a Hollywood talkie of imaginary English or Continental high life.

A grim spirit pervaded the grand house, accentuating the silence. These stately piles designed for crowds are like museums when denied them. Unoccupied they distil a haunting ghostliness. All such monuments have sprung like a tree from the soul of man, are but a reflection of that soul.

CHAPTER 24

It was a change-trains-cross-country journey back to town, and when I telephoned Sir Philmore Galstone's house at 10.30 he had not returned. When I rang at 11 o'clock I was informed that Sir Philmore had gone to Tattingwood Hall, summoned because Lord Tattingwood had taken a bad turn.

I could get no attention because Lord Tattingwood was so far gone that the little man at Supersnoring, as well as Sir Philmore, was occupied in transferring his allegiance to the heir.

Zarl was out at the theatre, I did not know which one, so could not extract her. I was exhausted and shaken beyond the comfort of food and sleep, and sat down to wait. I felt like wringing Percy's neck. Only for him I should never have gone to Tattingwood. Alone all day, he was delighted to see me, welcomed me flatteringly and kept up a clamour to be taken from his box. I released him, and threw myself on Zarl's divan bed, being unable to stand up. Percy took a position on my chest and put his arms around my neck. The warm furry presence had its comfort. He cuddled and gurgled so irresistibly that his execution was postponed for a time. Soon I found he required attention.

We had just settled down again when Zarl's key clicked in the lock. Someone was with her, saying good night. I feared she would invite him to take coffee, though it was 1.30. No, his footsteps retreated. Zarl turned on the light. 'Why aren't you in bed? Poor old Peanut, you look like a mouldy piece of bath soap. You've had a foul time I suppose. Did Swith die, or anything, while you were there?'

'No, but I nearly did.' I started to say something, and gave out.

Zarl to the rescue. I was put under an eider down. Percy was called a foul little humbug and tossed to his nest, where he had the savvy to pull his blanket over his head without a murmur.

'Something warm in your tummy; hot chocolate and toast.'

On this diet I regained myself surprisingly.

Zarl listened to my tale – well, Zarl has genius in listening. She never maddens the raconteur by interpolations. She was not horrified or surprised by Lord Tattingwood's confession. Inspector Frereton had constantly observed that if Lady Tattingwood could be got at, the mystery would be solved.

Zarl dismissed the accusations against me with an airiness that was inspiring. 'Pooh, the bally-whack old blackguard, you must put it down to his disease, and hop along.'

'It won't be pleasant to be suspected.'

'It might be the makings of you.' The adventurous champagne bubbles danced in her eyes. She was as effervescent as yeast. 'I'd snatch you from the noose and take you to see the ice break on the Lena and Indigirka. That was Professor Gilveray who saw me home. I've got him that his eyes are fairly bulging about discovering some of the natural mineral wealth in that belt. He's a geologist, and thinks a discovery like that might put the financial wheels in motion again, as gold did in past times. We want a live-stock fogey or two, and I've said you are a great cook, and they need me to take notes. It looks like a go. So cheer up! I'll hold your nose and pour a beaker of wine down your throat and force you to sleep. Nothing more now. We'll be in tighter places than this – I have been – just when drunken savates were going to, you know . . . but here I am still among the chased.'

Thus encouraged and fortified I fell asleep. In the morning, about eight, wakened by Percy, Zarl had the idea of telephoning Tattingwood Hall.

Lord Tattingwood was dead.

'Now,' I said, 'his document will be put in motion against me. I wonder if Scotland Yard will arrest me, and how I shall clear myself.'

'A fellow always has some friend,' said Zarl. We ruled Sir

Philmore Galstone out for this post. 'Showy old cad, more servile to the nobility than dedicated to medical science,' said Zarl. 'He was attending Clarice when she was taken to the Nursing Home, and if she was not deranged, as Swith says, why didn't the great pomposity discover it?'

I remembered the letter in my hand bag and produced it. On an inner envelope was scrawled '*To be opened without delay as soon as I peg out, but not before.*'

'He's just pegged out, so this is in the nick of time,' remarked Zarl, and broke the seal. A crisp bank note of a large denomination fell out, also another sealed envelope and a short note. The sealed envelope was addressed to, 'Clarice, my wife, by the hand of Miss Zarl Osterley.'

Zarl's note ran, 'I depend on you as one of the best scouts I ever knew to go to my wife immediately you hear of my death. She will need you. Persuade her to lean upon the facts in the letter herewith.'

'Wonder what's in this,' said Zarl. 'Wish I hadn't been reared to think that tapping letters was as foul as picking pockets. Perhaps it would save everything to know what is in this letter.'

She took Percy and me in a taxi and set off to the select Nursing Home where Clarice was. Fortunately it was in Greater London. 'I'll keep my family with me in case of dog and other inspectors,' she remarked.

'Philmore will not let you in.'

'Philmore is not prepared for my tactics,' she chuckled. 'While he is at Tattingwood, is my chance. He'll leave poor old Clarice high and dry for a bit while he digs in with the new Lord. Percy will be a topping help. Nursing mothers recently widowed are not in it with me and Percy for pull, as it acts with both sexes, and you will be at hand to take him if he becomes a nuisance.'

Zarl in her priceless furs, with her little monkey under her arm might have been a member of the Russian nobility or a celebrated 'it' actress, and so impressed the attendants. Her tactics worked up to the hilt and to the matron, and then upon the resident physician. That she was the person selected by Lord Tattingwood to come and break the sad news to his wife was not questioned. In a very short time she was in

Clarice's presence. The poor soul fell upon her friend's neck with a glad cry and weakly burst into tears, upbraiding her for forsaking her.

The attendants were for terming this hysteria, but Zarl said she would soon comfort her friend if left alone with her. She told her of her husband's death, which Clarice declared to be the vengeance of God, and Zarl said that as God demanded a monopoly of that business it had better be left to him, and instigated Clarice to open her letter.

It was short and rather cryptic:

> 'Better luck next throw old girl, I hope. Remember that on the night of the murder you met a sheeted figure, you did not know who it was, who flung you down the steps. That's all. The only important detail. Live and let live.'

Clarice wanted to leave the Home with Zarl, and failing that, piteously begged Zarl to remain with her. Zarl managed to retain the letter for safe keeping and resigned herself to stay with her friend, as she did not want the C.I.D. to get at her prematurely.

I had to go home alone with Percy Macacus Rhesus y Osterley, who was in roystering mood. He climbed up the wall with a bottle of ink and sat on the electric light bulbs. There he extracted the cork and scattered the liquid on the carpet. Lively measures with fresh milk were necessary. During these, Percy took opportunity to knock down and break a reading lamp, several dinner plates and a picture that Zarl valued. He was generously contributing diversion, but at length I caught him and tethered him, and did what I could to repair the damage.

When he was snugly in bed I fell a prey to my anxieties, and bethought me of the great Dr. Woodruff and his wife, and what a relief it would be to have them listen to my tale – as a medical secret.

Next day I sought them.

I revived when the doctor remained calm and unimpressed and did not seem to think that I was a homicide.

'It must be remembered that the disease from which Lord Tattingwood was suffering could have affected the brain.

163

Towards the end he would be in excruciating pain, and heavily drugged, and subject to mental delusions in keeping. In such circumstances innocent persons have been known to confess to crimes and misdemeanours they were incapable of committing. We know so little ... the effect of toxins on the mind and character ... we grope ... Everything Lord Tattingwood told you may have resulted from mental aberration ... and for his sins, however great or small, he has expiated ... I should not distress myself, if I were you, till you hear from Sir Philmore Galstone. He is eminently discreet.'

Our chief duty, Dr. Woodruff said, was to Lady Tattingwood, who must have suffered terribly and was the victim of circumstances. He had no doubt that she was in a state of nervous collapse from which she could recover with care.

The good doctor talked on to comfort me, in simple nonmedical language. He said he would make a few notes in case of accident, and then I could free myself from a feeling of responsibility in the matter. I suppressed for the time my gnawing fear of the document in the big envelope on the dying man's bed. What notice would be taken of that by the C.I.D.?

I told Dr. Woodruff the other leg of Lord Tattingwood's story – to use Yusuf's expression – concerning the accidental death of the superseded heir. Dr. Woodruff calmly remarked that that also was probably a figment of the dying man's brain. It seemed to me more like a figment of science to discredit it, but as Zarl said, 'When such figments are the right sort of garment for us, don't criticise them. The breakup of the present state of society is doing away with strongholds of privilege like Tattingwood in any case. Let's get on with our own washing.'

Our special laundry at that moment seemed to be the case of Clarice. With her wealth, there was no lack of laundresses, but Clarice clung to Zarl and gave signs of hysterical collapse when relegated to others. With Dr. Woodruff to pull official ropes, and the sanction of Cedd, there was no difficulty in gaining access to Clarice now that Swithwulf and his agents no longer held the pass.

Cedd arrived from the U.S.A. and furthered his stepmother's friendship with Zarl. In less than a week Zarl was allowed to bring her friend away from the Home where she had been a prisoner. She clung to Zarl piteously, so Zarl brought her straight to her little flat and Percy. The poor thing did not mind our humble way of life (and needless to report we immediately sewed a few frills on it in her honour) at all so long as she could be with us, and was assured of our help and sympathy. Fortunately there was a flat vacant near at hand which was speedily put in order with some of Clarice's own things, and she had the care of a nurse who was chosen by Dr. Woodruff.

Sir Philmore Galstone faded out of her picture without explosions. He was now, as Zarl had anticipated, busy impressing upon the new Lord Tattingwood the wonderful qualities of the boy heir, and doing all that would make him the popular physician to a great house, with the kind little fellow at Supersnoring faithfully echoing.

The King is dead! Long live the King! We all must live, even the insects.

'To cleanse us of this whole mess,' Zarl would expound, when we had a rare moment to ourselves, 'We must keep our minds concentrated on the Lena.' But one of the snags in mobilising scientists to struggle to the rich fields of northern Asia, was the invested fear of Sovietism. What was the use in making the world rich for Russia, if Russia would make the rich of the world poor by some pernicious experiment ethical and equitable distribution of the world's productiveness?

What indeed!

Amorous carrots dangling ahead of the donkeys of science were hardly sufficient to counteract this powerful astringent to the purse strings of those with capital to invest.

Inspector Frereton was no derelict of duty. As soon as practicable he had access to Lady Tattingwood in the interests of the law. But she rested secure in Zarl, leant on her like a child, and developed an immovable amount of self protection. Inspector Frereton already had a statement from her, to that she added a confused tale of meeting a horrid ghost and being so frightened that she had fallen down steps. She could not now remember how she received her severest injuries. When cross-questioned she conveniently lost her memory in a most convincing manner. Then her medical attendant and nurse would rescue her.

Cross-questioned as to why she had said nothing of the ghost in the first place she said that she had been to the room of her dear friend, Captain Stopworth, and had not stressed that because of giving pain to others, but now that her husband and Captain Stopworth both were dead, she was free to speak. In fact, said she, it was her dear husband who had most chivalrously suggested the acceptance of the broom to hide her story. She refused to make this statement more coherent.

'The doctors were sure that my mind had collapsed,' she said to Zarl. 'Let them reap the fruits of their own work from it now.'

'Good business!' chuckled Zarl. 'You stick to that. All things work together, or hang apart for good sometimes. Woodruff will be an earnest soul doing the will of his Lord; and you don't suppose Galstone will let any holes be made in his professional front without a stiff fight.'

A wife cannot be called upon to condemn her husband, and there seemed to be little upon which to re-open the case of the unsolved murder at Tattingwood Hall. Stopworth was dead! Tattingwood was dead; no one was accused. As to that document which I feared, Zarl said, 'Tush! It will get lost in the muddle somewhere, or if it does come to light, Woodruff and Galstone will establish it as evidence of mental aberration.'

I was the bystander punished for curiosity and listening-in because I had gone lightly to Tattingwood Hall to take care of a frolicsome monkey.

In putting her house in order, Zarl's attention fell upon Inspector Frereton littering the hob like a disused kettle and he was despatched to the dustman. 'He has nothing to tell us now,' she observed. 'We know more than he does, and he might worm things out in time if we permit him to be a cricket on the hearth.'

Inspector Frereton, finding himself discarded and also baulked of a spectacular solution of the Tattingwood case, turned mouldy. Zarl was nearly always out of the way with Clarice, and I as the bystander, again fell in for the discomfort. I don't think he knew himself how much of his spleen arose from disappointed gallant and how much from bootless sleuth.

He maintained that he had been sure from the first that the murder had been committed by someone of the household. 'It stands to reason that the old gentleman himself would have had a key to his own suite of rooms – that's how your door could have opened. I believe the old cock did it, but we could never get behind his position, and now he's dead.'

I opened my eyes in horrified astonishment, 'Nonsense! What a terrible idea!'

The Inspector spread himself a little, 'If you knew what we know, you wouldn't be surprised if one of the bishops was found out as a murderer. At the start I thought you or Miss Osterley might have done it.'

'But surely that was only until you knew us,' I said.

'Until all the clues against you gave out,' he retorted. 'And they haven't given out against *you* yet. You think you are very clever, and your friend thinks she is putting something over on us, but we knew she had that blue diamond, and when we nearly had her she had to crawl out of it through the monkey.'

'You surprise me,' I said.

'You think you are safe now, but you'll get daring – do something again, and then we shall be able to nab you at once,' was his parting thrust.

'Silly Peewit,' Zarl said when I reported this to her. 'A little knowledge has been very trying to him. I don't believe he *knew* that I had the blue diamond at all. He only guessed it because it was so long coming to light.'

'Did you have the blue diamond?' I asked, genuinely astonished.

'Of course I did. That Peewit of a Jimmy handed it to me in the commotion while Ydonea was yelping, and I had it all the time.'

'All through the searching?'

'Of course.'

'You never told me.'

'No, when it ended in that frightful tragedy the thing became a burden, and what was the good of doubling it.'

'But how did it start?'

'I can tell you the whole thing in five minutes . . . It started as a genuine lark, and a publicity stunt. We never thought we'd get through with the thing. The Elephant Hunter and Jimmy were to procure the gems, and I was to be the fence. I got the blue diamond all right, and stuck to it, as I said it would be easy to do . . . And then poor Stopworth was killed, and Jimmy gone without explanation or anything, and I found myself in one of the fixes of my life. I did not know whether I had been used as a dupe, or what. Silence seemed the safest thing for me. I had no right to drag you into the worry of it. You have a desperately intense strain in you, and too much old-fashioned conscience. I thought of tossing the bally thing away a dozen times, but somehow I could not do it when it came to the point . . . the worship of money is in us all, I suppose . . . Then I saw our premises had been searched in our absence, and would be again. I might be seized any day and searched personally . . . Well, to cut the cackle, the diamond seemed to get bigger and bigger, and to have a spotlight indicating its position, no matter where I put it. Then you came along quite innocently with your idea that it could still be in Percy, and I saw my deliverance was near . . . I had a colossical struggle to get it down the poor little beggar's throat . . . He's tremendously clever at not swallowing anything he dislikes. You know the remainder. I never expected it to go through with so little scandal . . . but you see how your good faith helped . . . The story would look very lame coming out now, so silence altogether is best, besides, the diamond had no real bearing on the murder.'

I agreed with her in this. 'Where did you secrete the diamond while being searched?'

'Ah, that was so simple, I never thought it would act. I'll share that secret with you when we are watching the ice break on the Lena,' she chuckled.

The Yard shelved the case with commendable circumspection. Some wise heads must have decided that no service would be rendered Church or State by re-opening a doubtful case to punish no criminal, but merely to throw a shadow on the lineage of the new Lord Tattingwood, a worthy and dull citizen for ever involved in good works such as preserving the beauty of rural England or brightening the slums; nor upon the Hon. Cedd Spillbeans, now one of the hopes of the British film industry.

Swithwulf had escaped to a higher tribunal, or to nothingness, or Nirvana. Lady Tattingwood could scarcely be arrainged as accessory, nor for concealing evidence, when several high medical authorities had certified her into a mental home where her attempts to communicate with the outer world had been intercepted. She might have had a case had she cared to pursue it.

All that she wished to pursue, however, was the case of her child, and this she would now be at liberty to do under dignified and feasible cover.

There was no difficulty in tracing Clarice Denise Stopworth, or Lesserman as she might be in law. Inspector Frereton was able to help there, and recovered some of his equanimity in service.

The child had been at a select girls' school at Rotherhythe till the Christmas following Stopworth's death, when the fees had become too much for Stopworth's aged and valiant mother. Mrs. Stopworth Sr. had been in her son's confidence from the beginning. It was she who had received the child, a small bundle, from his arms in 1917, and without quibble had wrapt it in her affection. The road was now clear for Clarice.

She never wished to see Tattingwood Hall again, and the remnant of her fortune was ample for her to retreat to some more simple way of living, preferably abroad, till her case should be eclipsed by a newer sensation. Dr. Woodruff advised a long sea voyage as the best way for her to recuperate and to escape acquaintances whose curiosity might be trying.

Upon the suggestion of Zarl, she decided to take a trip to Australia, and to invite the younger Clarice Denise and her grandmother to accompany her. This was prevalent Imperial good form, engendered by the crusade to stay in our own back yards and travel about our own runs, so gloriously far flung, and thus keep our sterling in the family.

During the delightful weeks at sea involved, Clarice was to become acquainted with the child of her middle age, of her first and only romance. Later, if the girl showed herself amenable, her mother could legally adopt her. Thus the poor woman had a chance of mending her tattered life. Much would depend upon the girl's character as she developed.

CHAPTER 25

'A great clearing-up, like a jig-saw puzzle,' remarked Zarl, 'but it is not taking us to the Lena. I'll set off with Percy one of these days if no other gentleman will accompany me.'

Then it looked as if seeing the crocodiles laze in the regions of the Limpopo would be likelier than icebreaking on the Lena. The Elephant Hunter, by name of Brodribb, wrote again. He sent one note to the Bishop of Donchester and another to Cedd Spillbeans. He stated that he had more definite news from wild ivory hunters, of the man who had fallen out of a great eagle in the sky somewhere between Ubangui and Uganda, or names like that. He thought this might be Jimmy Wengham. If not, it was some other air man whom it would be the sportsmanlike thing to rescue. According to garbled tales, this man was being held as a wizard or devil or something. The Elephant Hunter was ready to lead a party, but was now low in funds, and it would be a costly expedition.

Cedd was inclined to believe that it was not Jimmy's route, but the poor old Bishop was full of hope and enthusiasm. He communicated with Ydonea, who had just returned from Northern Canada to New York. Headlines soon staggered under her name and exploits. Money must be raised at once to send an expedition to rescue Jimmy. Cedd was suspicious that it was a scheme of the Elephant Hunter to glorify himself and be financed. Cedd's recent experiences led him to suspect publicity in all things.

Ydonea had found a lever at last with which to get Zarl into her exploits. She promised to think of a Siberian film with wonderful Russian methods, with Zarl participating in some form, if Zarl would only use her influence to induce Cedd to have a film of Ydonea at Tattingwood Hall. She wanted this to be conventional, with oodles of 'it' and platinum vamping, and Percy as a novelty in many star shots. Percy was to be the little something extra which makes a play of any class a success. 'And then,' said Ydonea, 'I guess I'll be at the end of the platinum blonde business; and two films, one of the Lena and the other of the Limpopo would be a nice change.'

The Tattingwoods were willing to have the Hall used for the patriotic purpose of aiding British industry, and also to help with the death duties. There was no trouble about an author to provide a story. The one that had happened was to be used. A skilled continuity writer was to shape it. Everything was to spin on Ydonea's platinum 'it.'

And I was to be in it Ho, Ho! and yo-yo as Percy's attendant!!! and publicity expert!!!

Jimmy Wengham, or his impersonator, would scour the world for love of blonde beauty.

The Elephant Hunter would be in the wilderness for the same reason; Yusuf was a Rajah in disguise as a chauffeur for the same reason, and the handsome Inspector was killed because of God knows what by the devil knows whom. But that would not matter to a story depending on 'continuity' instead of mere coherence or cause or effect, now so sedately out of vogue. It would be useful to furnish the screen in those places of refuge for adolescents in the throes of their own 'it,' or those others, recovered from the distemper but who nevertheless require some irritant to save them from melancholia by making thought impossible.

We are to begin this picture immediately. The idea of doing a serious jungle film of the expedition in search of Jimmy Wengham has caught the imagination of the public. The rumours of a man who tumbled out of the sky in central Africa have increasing body. The Elephant Hunter's despatches are given prominence in the news. Interest has been aroused in scientific circles. The Imperial Geographical Club is moving in the matter.

'I'm longing to see the Elephant Hunter again,' said Zarl.

'He is almost a real man. Do you know that he never even asked me if I managed to get the diamond that night. Just shut up. That makes him the strongest he- or she-man I ever heard of. Not a bad old cow at all ... Ah, ha, I've just thought of the sex interest for the expedition film ...'

I looked up expectantly – over a book by Norman Lindsay.

Zarl was overtaken with convulsions of mirth. 'Ydonea shall vamp the Elephant Hunter in the wilds. Picture it!'

'What about Jimmy's part?'

'He can chase butterflies with a net for all I care. Or, he can fall in love with a savage princess, who has saved his life, *and stick to her*. That will be a novelty after the flocks of white men who always kite off and forsake the poor little darkies or brownies who have saved their lives. Ho! Ho! and yo-yo, sure enough. I can hardly wait to see the Elephant Hunter doing a twenty horse power vamp suction kiss.'

'I hope it will be sufficient compensation for the skeets.'

'You have an ungainly habit of thinking of practical things.'

'Just think how useful Percy Macacus Rhesus y Osterley will be among the ignorant uncultured monkeys.'

'You are taking him?'

'Of course.'

I am limbering my fortitude in readiness.

Clarice is happy on the P. and O. cruise, and adores the Australians. She writes that she has been guest of honour at countless affairs. She does not know why she is honoured nor what the functions represent, but describes them all as richly furnished with cakes and smothered in flowers. She thinks she has opened things.

Zarl says that Australian tea-parties full of flutter and misplaced deference to a title, and free from any mental stimulation, are just the routine to soothe Clarice's exacerbated nerves and to recall her wandering wits.

Young Clarice Denise is ecstatic about the surfing.

I too am now quite at ease about the Tattingwood case and have returned to the perusal of Bernard Shaw in thanksgiving. Some days since, Cedd Spillbeans brought me a parcel which he said came to me by the wish of his father.

I recognised the big linen envelope which had lain on Lord

Tattingwood's coverlet, and did not break the seal till Zarl and I were behind locked doors.

The packet disclosed the dirk, still bound with Lord Tattingwood's handkerchief. The little parcel contained the pink pearl set in a platinum pin of Tiffany workmanship. The small sealed envelope was addressed in Lord Tattingwood's hand, in ink, and there was an almost undecipherable scrawl in pencil:

'Ha, ha! I had a trump after all. The story I told was true except for the bit I said you did. I did that myself. The dirk went home like a bird. You can do the filling in like the old johnnies who restore the noses on statues. Cheerio!'

The note inside was formal, evidently written at some earlier time:

'Lord Tattingwood asks Miss Carrington to accept the enclosed tie-pin and South African dagger as a souvenir of her first visit to Tattingwood Hall, which no doubt she would have enjoyed less if Lord Tattingwood had enjoyed it more.'